SHELTER

SHELTER

BETH COOLEY

DELACORTE PRESS

Published by Delacorte Press
an imprint of Random House Children's Books
a division of Random House, Inc.
New York

Delacorte Press and colophon are registered trademarks
of Random House, Inc.

www.randomhouse.com/teens
Educators and librarians, for a variety of teaching tools,
visit us at www.randomhouse.com/teachers

Library of Congress Cataloging-in-Publication Data
Cooley, Beth.
    Shelter / Beth Cooley.—1st ed.
        p. cm.
    Summary: Following her father's death and the discovery of his debts,
high school sophomore Lucy moves with her mother and brother from
their upper-middle-class neighborhood into a homeless shelter where she
tries to come to terms with her new life.
    ISBN-13: 978-0-385-73330-4 (hardcover)—
    ISBN-13: 978-0-385-90347-9 (glb edition)
    ISBN-10: 0-385-73330-5 (hardcover)—
    ISBN-10: 0-385-90347-2 (glb edition)
    [1. Shelters for the homeless—Fiction. 2. Homeless persons—
Fiction. 3. Family life—Fiction.] I. Title.
PZ7.C7765She 2006
[Fic]—dc22
2005036535

The text of this book is set in 12-point Goudy.
Printed in the United States of America

10 9 8 7 6 5 4 3 2 1
First Edition

Thanks to Nadine Van Stone and to the women at St. Margaret's Shelter, whose lives and stories were an inspiration.

For Dan

The night we got here it was snowing hard. Big wet flakes splattered on the windshield as Mom pulled the car up close to the front door. She reached under her seat and popped the trunk open.

"Grab as much stuff as you can," she told me, and unlatched Jimmy's seat belt.

"Where should I take it?" I asked.

"They'll let us know once we get inside."

I zipped my coat up against the blowing snow and hauled a suitcase and backpack out of the trunk while Mom pulled my little brother out of the car. Holding him on her hip, she pressed the button on the call box at the heavy door. I could hear a phone ringing through the intercom. Then a woman's voice answered and asked for Mom's name.

"Cindy Durbin," Mom said, and the door unlocked with a loud click.

I dropped my suitcase and backpack inside and ran back to the car to grab a garbage bag full of towels and a couple of pillows. For a second it felt like I was unpacking at the cabin we used to rent on Priest Lake every August, but only for a second. This was no vacation. I lugged everything through the front door and added it to the pile of suitcases, backpacks, and boxes of Jimmy's toys.

"That's it," I told Mom, and looked around at the place where we were going to live.

Sofas and chairs were arranged in small groups; cheap silk flower baskets and lamps stood on the end tables. If you didn't know you had just entered St. Agatha's Shelter for Women and Children, you might think you'd stepped into the lobby of a budget motel. The kind of room people used but no one owned—like a waiting room. Here we would wait for things to get better.

"No one seems to be around," I said, wondering who had answered the call box and unlocked the door.

Mom put Jimmy down and unzipped his coat. His cheeks were red from the cold, and he swayed a little with sleepiness. She cleared her throat loudly.

A woman with heavy glasses and gray hair poked her head out of a doorway. "Cindy Durbin?" she asked.

"I'm Cindy," Mom replied. "And this is my daughter, Lucy. And Jimmy, my son. He's small for five," she added. I could tell she was nervous.

"I'm Paula Fairchild. Welcome to St. Agatha's." The

woman held out her hand, and after a second's hesitation Mom shook it. "We were expecting you earlier."

"I'm so sorry. We didn't get everything together as soon as I had hoped to, and then we needed to stop for dinner." Mom was smiling so hard it looked painful. The truth was we could have arrived hours ago. By ten that morning we had checked out of the motel where we'd spent the last week. Then we'd hauled some boxes to the storage space we rented near the airport. Then we'd gone to the cemetery to make sure the silk poinsettias weren't covered with snow, and we'd stood in the cold for a little while looking at the grave. After we'd eaten at McDonald's, Mom had taken us to the library. While I read to Jimmy and tried to keep him entertained by drawing with him, she'd searched through reference books on career opportunities. I don't know what she was thinking. Maybe that she would find some kind of answer to her problem, our problem, in one of those thick books.

"That's all right," Paula said. "You must be ready to get settled in. Let me show you where you'll be staying."

We followed her back through the lobby, past a large kitchen and up some stairs. I could hear people talking behind some of the doors, muffled laughter, a baby crying, but nobody else was in sight.

"Please make as little noise as possible while you get unpacked. Quiet hours at St. Agatha's are from nine p.m. to seven a.m." Paula unlocked a door and handed the key to Mom. "Here we are. Room number twelve."

Unlike the lobby, nothing about room 12 suggested a motel, budget or otherwise. It was long and narrow with beige walls. At one end stood two beds, a double and a single. At the other end, a desk and chest of drawers. None of the furniture went together. The carpet was nappy, and there were no curtains at the windows, only mini-blinds.

"Here's the closet," Paula said. "The bathroom is right down the hall. The kitchen is open all the time. We ask that you clean up after yourselves as soon as you finish. We don't want to attract mice or insects." Mom shuddered. "Did you bring any food that needs to be put away?"

Mom shook her head. "I didn't have time."

"That's okay. There's cereal in the Food Bank pantry for breakfast. The pantry door is clearly marked. Everything else belongs to someone, so make sure you don't eat anything that has somebody's name on it."

"Thank you," Mom said softly. She was staring around the room. I could feel her hopelessness, could almost smell it like perfume on her skin.

"Well, that's about it," Paula said, pushing her glasses up her nose. "Tomorrow you'll get the grand tour. If you need anything, just give a shout. The phone there by the bed calls the office. You don't have an outside line, but you can receive and place calls downstairs. Sleep well."

As soon as Paula closed the door, Mom sat down on the bare mattress. "I'm so sorry I had to bring you here," she said, her voice wavering. "I never dreamed we'd end up in a place like this."

"We need to make the beds," I said, pulling sheets out of a plastic garbage bag. Crying would do no good.

Talking would do no good. The only way to get through this was not to dwell on it. "Here are the double sheets." I threw them to her a little harder than I meant to. "I'll make up the single bed."

She stood up wearily and blew her nose. With a sigh she stretched the fitted sheet across the thin mattress. I made the narrow bed I would sleep in, remembering my canopy bed in our old house, my ruffled lavender pillows. This is not my bed, I thought as I tucked in the corners. I would sleep in it, but it would never be mine.

The next morning I woke up at six o'clock to the sound of country music. The clock radio in the room next door beeped over a whiny voice and a twanging guitar. Jimmy sat up in bed and called for Mom like he did every morning. He didn't seem to realize she was lying right next to him, her head under the pillow.

"It's all right, baby," she said, and pulled him to her. Jimmy's curly red hair stood up in tufts all over his head, and she tried to smooth it down. She looked like absolute hell. The gray in her hair was showing; she hadn't had it touched up in months. Her eyes were puffy, and her cheeks were slack. She looked more like Jimmy's grandmother than his mom.

"What happened to quiet hours?" I asked, and gazed around the room noticing things I hadn't last night. The bent mini-blinds, the red crayon marks on the wall, the scarred chest of drawers looked even worse in the daylight. "How can we possibly stay here?"

"We'll get used to it," she said. "Everything's going to be all right." But she knew as well as I did that was just something people said when everything was all wrong. And it wasn't going to get better anytime soon.

I got dressed before I headed for the bathroom, even though I really had to pee. I wasn't going out into the hallway in my pajamas, not in front of a bunch of strangers. I took my soap, towel and toothbrush and knocked on the bathroom door.

"It's open," a woman in a short blue nightgown said as she walked past me down the hall. "Just go on in."

The bathroom was huge, like the one in the college dorm I stayed in for tennis camp last summer. When I had used it the night before I had been too tired to pay attention. Now I looked around carefully. It seemed clean enough, but I wished I'd put on my slippers. The floor tiles were cold and clammy and I imagined germs crawling under my toenails. The shower stalls had curtains, and the toilet stalls had doors, but I already knew I'd never have any real privacy in here. This was no place for facials or pedicures or long soaks in the tub, which didn't even exist. And where was Jimmy supposed to go? Was there a bathroom for little boys, or did they just come on in with their mommies?

Deciding to skip my shower, I turned on the faucet and waited for the water to run warm. Looking at myself in the mirror over the sink, I ran my fingers through my curly blond hair. It was completely wild. I hadn't had it cut in months.

I went downstairs to the kitchen. I guess I should have told Mom where I was going, but she'd find me. She had looked like she was on the verge of tears when I left our room, and I just couldn't deal with that first thing this morning. Every time she broke down I went through it too. But all inside. And then I got mad. Mad at myself for not being able to cope. Mad at her for being so helpless. Then guilty.

How had we ended up in a homeless shelter? And how would we get out?

2

If the shelter's living room looked like a cheap motel lobby and the bathroom looked like it belonged in a dorm, the kitchen looked like an appliance store, with six stoves and six refrigerators lined up along the walls and eight foldout tables and chairs in the center. Each family at St. Agatha's was assigned a stove and refrigerator to share with two other families. The tables were open to anyone. Nobody else was in the kitchen, but a coffeemaker gurgled and hissed on the counter. The smell made me realize how hungry I was. The cheeseburger I'd eaten the day before hadn't been enough, and I'd dreamed about Mom's spinach lasagna, beef Stroganoff, chicken divan, the kind of food she hadn't made in months.

I took a box of cereal from the Food Bank pantry. On the box was printed KORN KRISPS. These weren't even cornflakes. Were we really reduced to eating generic cereal? In one of the refrigerators I found a carton of milk that didn't have someone's name on it. Skim, but it would have to do. It was after seven o'clock, and the kitchen was beginning to fill up with other residents. Some of them stared at me. Most ignored me. Nobody talked to me. Not until I poured milk on my Korn Krisps.

"Is that milk yours?" a girl about my age asked in a rough voice. She stood with her hands on her hips, her blue eyes narrowed.

"What?" I was so startled, I spilled some milk on the table.

"I said, is that your milk? Or does it maybe have some-body's name on it?"

I turned the carton around, looking. The room had gotten quiet, and everyone was watching us.

"Check the bottom," she said. Her brown hair was growing out of a bad dye job. Her sweater looked about two sizes too small, and she had a row of silver hoops go-ing up her ear.

"Oh. It says Crystal. I'm sorry. I didn't see it."

"Look harder next time," she said, taking the carton from me.

"I said I'm sorry." All of a sudden I'd had enough of her, enough of this place and fake cereal and skim milk. "You want it back?" I picked up my bowl. She flinched like she thought I was going to throw it at her. Then she rolled her eyes and walked away.

I wasn't hungry anymore. The soggy flakes floated in the bowl, and even though I tried my best to stop them, tears flooded my eyes. All around me women poured cereal for their kids, stuck Pop-Tarts in toasters. How could I possibly live here? If I were a couple of years older, I could live on my own. I could get a job, rent a place, figure out some way to go to college. But I was stuck. In less than six months I'd moved from a five-bedroom house with my own bathroom and TV to room number 12 at a homeless shelter. I'd gone from croissants and cappuccino to Korn Krisps. And it sucked.

"Want one?" A box of donuts appeared under my nose. I looked up. Across the table a large woman with short black hair, squinty brown eyes and crooked teeth smiled at me. "You like Krispy Kreme?"

"Yeah. I guess."

"Go on, take one. They're a day old, but you can't hardly tell." I took a donut. "When'd you move in?"

"Last night," I said.

"Well, you'll get used to things around here. And people. Like Crystal Brick." She nodded toward the girl with the milk carton, who was trying to feed a baby runny cereal. "You got to stand your ground with her. And you did. You'll do okay with Crystal."

"I didn't know it was hers."

"Course not. How could you? I think she puts her name on the bottoms of things just to stir up some excitement. But she's all right once you get to know her." She licked glazed sugar from the corner of her mouth. "I'm Jan."

"I'm Lucy," I said. "Thanks for the donut."

"Have all you want. I sure don't need to be eating them, and neither does Carlos. Hey, Carlos!" she yelled across the room. "You and Alonzo want a Krispy Kreme?"

Carlos was only seven, Jan said, but he was already up to his mom's shoulder, and heavy to match. He had coarse black hair that stuck up in cowlicks, and bright black eyes and a quick smile like his mother. At the sight of the donuts he lumbered across the kitchen.

"You new?" he asked, and grinned at me. I nodded. "We been here over a year," he said, as if he were proud of it. Then he took a donut in each hand and ran back to his friend, a dark skinny little kid who looked about the same age.

"I got to get them two ready for school. The bus will be here in twenty minutes." Jan stood up and called to Carlos and Alonzo again. "So, you here with your mama or with a baby?" she asked.

"With my mom," I answered, trying to hide the shock I felt. How could she think I had a kid of my own? Did I look like that kind of person? Jan must have read my expression, because she smiled and shook her head.

"Crystal there, she's got a baby. Six months old. She's not but seventeen. How old are you?"

"I'll be sixteen next month."

"In February? You a Pisces?" she asked.

"Aquarius," I said.

"Me, I'm a Libra. Means I'm balanced," she said, and then she laughed like that was the funniest thing she'd heard in a while.

We got the tour of St. Agatha's Shelter later that morning from the director, Rachel Pratt. Rachel was younger than Paula, who was the night supervisor, and wore her auburn hair in a long braid. When she talked to you, she looked right into your eyes. When she smiled, you smiled too. There was something peaceful about Rachel, and right away I knew if I ever needed anything she'd be the one I'd go to.

"Just stop me if you've got any questions," she said as she led us downstairs to the basement. She showed us a large playroom, storage areas and a room full of racks and boxes of clothes that normal people didn't want anymore. At a glance I could tell most of the clothes were pretty awful. Cheap knits and bad colors. A laundry room, a makeshift library and three computers were in the basement too.

"And here's where the vacuum cleaners and cleaning supplies are stored," Rachel said, opening a closet door. "We'll get you signed on to a crew when we go back upstairs."

"Crew?" Mom repeated.

"For cleaning duty. It only takes a few hours a week since everyone pitches in."

Back on the main floor Rachel showed us a couple of meeting rooms along with the office, the kitchen and the staff apartment where Paula slept.

"Residents gather in the meeting rooms for group sessions and classes," Rachel explained. "We encourage the adult residents to attend at least two classes a week."

"What kind of classes?" Mom asked timidly.

"Substance abuse prevention, domestic violence, parenting. Also résumé writing, painting, journaling. Last summer we had a quilting class. Some of the women made beautiful quilts," Rachel said. "There's one hanging in the living room. Did you notice it?"

"I don't think I did," Mom said politely. She tangled her fingers together and smiled. I knew the idea of meeting twice a week with the other residents was making her anxious. It was obvious that no one else at St. Agatha's was like my mother. Cindy Durbin, former member of the racquet club, the country club, the Junior League, Bentley Academy PTA and Andover Hills Neighborhood Association. Who every Friday got a manicure at Spa Esprit, who every second Thursday got her hair touched up at Claude's. Every winter we had gone skiing in Canada. Every summer we had rented a lake cabin. We'd had digital cable and cell phones and e-mail. Once.

"The classes provide structured activity. It's a good place to get to know the other residents, as well," Rachel explained. "And of course you'll start WorkFirst as soon as we can get the paperwork done."

"WorkFirst?" Mom repeated.

"Job training. You'll enroll in classes at the community college."

Mom nodded. Although she'd had a year of college before she got married, she had never worked a day in her married life. Her place was in the home, Dad had said. At least until Jimmy was in middle school. After Dad died, she'd gotten a part-time job at a bookstore, but it closed. She'd applied for other jobs—cashier, secretary—but nobody was hiring fortyish women with no experience.

"You're already fixed for food stamps, and Medicaid will kick in soon. You'll be eligible for housing assistance eventually, but some other things need to fall into place first. Lucy, we can put you on the free-lunch program at school."

Mom nodded, but I don't think she was really listening. I was trying to deal with the fact that I'd be a free-lunch student. Free lunch was for losers, for people like Crystal Brick. Not people like me.

When the tour was over, Mom went back upstairs with Jimmy. As soon as he'd woken up, he had pulled the blanket off my bed and tented it over the desk and chair. He'd crawled under the blanket with his bucket of LEGOs. When I lifted the corner, he politely told me to close the door to his house. His first instinct, his first job as a kid in a homeless shelter, was to build himself a house and stay in it.

That might work for Jimmy, but I couldn't stand to stay inside. I wandered out into the fenced courtyard just off the kitchen and breathed in the cold sharp air. It felt good to be outside, a gray sky above me and snow under my feet, but the courtyard was too small. Rachel had explained that the tall wrought iron fence was there for the same reason the call box was on the front door, to protect the residents from anybody who might want to harm them: husbands, ex-husbands, boyfriends. Dealers. Pimps. It was very cold and, since most of the kids and some of the moms were at school that morning, very quiet there in the courtyard.

I had to go back to school on Monday. I'd been out since Christmas break. Mom had let me have an extra week off to adjust to our move. Only three more days. I'd been dreading it, but compared to sitting around St. Agatha's it was starting to look pretty good.

• • •

"Where are you going?" Mom asked as I took my coat from the small closet and pulled on my boots.

"For a walk," I said, wishing she'd just be quiet and let me go. She was sitting next to Jimmy's blanket house, reading Dr. Seuss. Jimmy's curly orange head stuck out from under the blanket, and he looked up at me with wide gray eyes.

"But you don't know the neighborhood," Mom protested. "You might get lost."

"I won't."

"You're mad at me, aren't you, Lucy? You blame me for being here."

"I'm not mad at you, and I don't blame you," I said. "I don't blame anybody."

"You know we wouldn't be here if there were any other way," Mom said. Her voice was starting to get shaky, like she was about to cry again. And I couldn't stand tears.

"I know, Mom. It's not your fault." I tried to keep my voice neutral as I opened the door. "I'll be back in a little while."

"Be careful. Stay close by. Don't—"

I closed the door on her worries. She was right. It wasn't her fault. And I didn't blame her. How could I? The only person to blame for us landing in a homeless shelter was my father. And he was dead.

As I walked down the sidewalk away from St. Agatha's, light snow was falling. The sky was that strange white gray of winter mornings, and the banked snow was faintly blue. I turned up my coat collar and tried to picture my father. Instead of images I could only think of words to describe him—strong, tall, copper-brown hair,

15

gray eyes. I couldn't see his face anymore, only the shape of a man pushing a lawn mower across the backyard. That was what he'd been doing the last time I saw him. I could still smell the new-cut grass, still feel the deck railing warm under my hand, but I couldn't remember his face.

He had died over five months ago, after his jeep slid off a bluff. The accident was a shock. Losing him two days later on the operating table was much worse. Over the next four days Mom had managed to plan a funeral, pay for a casket and a headstone, even comfort his friends. She assured Jimmy and me how much he'd loved us.

And then she broke down completely. For a week she couldn't get out of bed. Somehow I kept myself and Jimmy fed and clean until she pulled herself together enough to get dressed.

On August third she came downstairs. I remember the date because we were supposed to go to Priest Lake that day. First Mom called and canceled our reservations, forfeiting our deposit, which we could have used a lot more than she realized at the time. Then she flipped through the stack of mail that had been growing on the dining room table. She wrote checks, paid bills, called the bank. Then she called a lawyer.

That whole afternoon she was gone. Then the whole next day. When she came home, she ordered pizza, something I couldn't remember her ever doing before. My mom sees takeout as a moral failing. And Dad wouldn't have stood for it. Only home cooking for him. But that night she set the table, poured herself a glass of wine and opened the pizza box. Then she told me we were going to move.

"Move where?" I asked.

"I've found a nice place to rent until we get back on our feet."

"You mean we're selling the house?"

"We can't afford it anymore."

"But Dad built this house!" My father, a contractor, had let Mom pick out the lot in the Andover Hills subdivision. He had let her include anything she wanted in the design—a granite island in the kitchen, a slate floor in the mudroom, a balcony off the master suite.

"He built it, but we don't own it," she said. "We have a mortgage that we can't afford. And a lot of debt that I didn't know about." She had started upstairs with her glass of wine. She hadn't touched the pizza. I ran up the stairs behind her.

At her bedroom door she turned to face me. "I've found a duplex in the Randolf High School district. Randolf's a good school," she said, and I suddenly realized I wouldn't be going back to Bentley Academy. I'd be going to the big public high school downtown.

"But what about my friends?" I cried.

"You'll keep in touch with them." She sighed. "There's no other way, Lucy."

"Can't we just buy a smaller house?" I couldn't believe we'd be renting. And a duplex? Everyone I knew lived in nice houses with three-car garages and landscaping.

"We simply have nothing to buy one with," she said. "It's complicated. Your father put a lot into the business. He made some bad investments. He borrowed."

"Everybody borrows!" I said. "What about life insurance?"

"He . . . it wasn't paid. Mr. Monath, the lawyer, is looking into it, but things are a mess."

"Are you saying we're broke? Like, bankrupt?"

"I can't talk about this right now, Lucy," she'd said. "I need to lie down."

The snow was falling harder now. The street in front of St. Agatha's curved up a hill and lost itself in a neighborhood of small houses and apartment buildings. I trudged along its unshoveled sidewalks, taking in the battered cars and sagging fences that edged the yards. A couple of faceless snowmen stood in the yards, their stick arms angled crazily. This was a part of town I didn't know, a part of town I never would have dreamed of walking through a month ago.

Now I lived here.

The first weekend at St. Agatha's was like something out of a bad TV movie. One family got kicked out because the mom had weed in her room. Child Protective Services came to get her children. The skinny black kid, Alonzo, broke his arm sliding on icy concrete. Some kind of bug was running its course through the kids. Jimmy had been up sick all night, and I'd gotten no sleep.

Then on Sunday morning Mom was called down to the office for a random drug test.

"I have never done drugs in my life," she protested when Rachel handed her a plastic cup. She was more indignant than embarrassed, and I have to admit I was glad to see some fire in her eyes for a change. Rachel explained that random drug tests and room searches were shelter

policy. Just like no candles, no perfume and no pets. N
private phone lines. Mom took the cup and marched in
the bathroom.

"Weekends are always rough," Jan said. "But usually not
this rough." She held out a bag of Doritos, and I took
a handful.

I was sitting at one of the foldout tables in the kitchen,
trying to read. I had a lot of catching up to do before I
went back to school, and it was hard to find a quiet place
to concentrate. I refused to spend any more time in the
room. I couldn't stand the bent blinds and nappy carpet
and crayon-marked walls any longer. The library was being used for a domestic violence prevention session, and
the computer room was packed with women and kids doing homework. A lot of the women went to Cottonwood
Falls Community College, and they seemed to take getting a degree pretty seriously. That and a job would be
their ticket out of the shelter. Crystal Brick had been at
one of the computers typing furiously. She looked up at
me standing in the doorway, like she dared me to enter.
Screw her, I thought, and left.

"How's Alonzo's arm?" I asked, searching for something to say to Jan.

"It'll be all right. His mama about broke his other one
once she found out he'd hurt himself again." She laughed.
"That boy is always getting busted up."

I don't know why she thought this was funny. Maybe
that's what living in a homeless shelter too long does for a
person—makes everything a joke.

"You reading up for school?" she asked.

I nodded, and closed my social studies book. I could tell Jan was in the mood for a chat, and I didn't know how to escape.

"Yeah, you didn't strike me as the kind that'd drop out, and your mama didn't strike me as the homeschool type either. You worried?"

"What about?"

"Going back."

"No," I lied. "Why should I be?"

Jan shrugged. "I dropped out soon as I turned sixteen. Couldn't stand sitting in a desk all day long. I finally got my GED couple years ago. Twenty years late, but better late than never. I'm going to finish my certificate in early childhood education from the community college, and then I'm gone. Been at St. Agatha's too long."

"How'd you end up here?" I asked.

"The cops found a meth lab in the basement," Jan said. "You know, methamphetamine? Talk about poison. Anyway, CPS took Carlos, and the police arrested my so-called boyfriend. Lucky for me I wasn't there at the time. I was charged with accessory, but my lawyer cut a deal that sent that son of a bitch I was living with to jail—pardon my language—and got my charges dropped. I ended up here and got clean. Then I got Carlos back." She picked a piece of Dorito out of her teeth. "Once I get a job and a place to live, we're out of here."

"Oh. Well." What was I supposed to say to that? That I was glad she escaped felony charges? That things could only get better? Jeez! What kind of people was I living with? Meth addicts and criminals and practitioners of child neglect?

"A lot of people have gotten clean here and are staying clean," Jan went on. "A lot of them lost their children and got them back. There's some backsliders, but you got to expect that. Some people never learn. But that's not everybody's story."

"What's Crystal's story?" I asked. Not that I cared, really.

"Crystal Brick? Got pregnant, grandma kicked her out, came here, had her baby. I'm leaving out a lot. You ought to ask her sometime."

Right, I thought. I was planning to stay as far away from Crystal Brick as I could. Soon Mom would have Dad's finances in order, and we'd be back in a house. I'd be back at Bentley and would never have to talk to people like Jan and Crystal again.

That would be my story. I had to believe that. Or I couldn't keep getting out of bed.

3

Monday morning I walked the two miles to Randolf High School. Mom said she'd drive me, but I wanted some time alone, just to think things through. I planned to get there just as the bell rang so I wouldn't have to stand in the halls by myself. Although I had gone to Randolf for the whole fall semester, I hadn't gotten to know people. I didn't really want to. At Bentley Academy I'd had lots of friends, but I never saw them anymore. They had all come to Dad's funeral, of course, mostly with their parents. Their moms had brought casseroles and sent flowers, but after that we kind of lost touch. Even before we moved to the duplex, most of them had quit calling.

Having a family member die makes you special, but in a not-so-good way. When my best friends, Kari and

Amanda, and some others came over a few days after the funeral, they didn't know what to talk about. They didn't want to ask anything about my dad, or about Mom not leaving her room, but they didn't want to talk about the ordinary summer stuff they were doing either, the parties and trips to the lake and hanging out at Kari's pool. Everything I'd been missing. Dad's death was the elephant in the room, only more like a rhinoceros—ugly and scary. Everybody could see it, but no one was supposed to mention it. Since I suddenly owned a rhinoceros, my friends and I had nothing in common. We just sat there talking about this movie we'd all gone to before the accident, and then they left.

Once we moved out of our house, I never saw them again. Maybe some of it was my fault. I didn't always return their calls, but what could I do? When Amanda had her Sweet Sixteen at the country club, I couldn't get a new dress or a decent present. So I told her I was sick. When Kari asked me to spend fall break with her family on the Oregon coast, I didn't have the money for shopping and entertainment and eating out. Kari's parents probably would have paid for everything if they'd known how bad things were. But how could we tell people we were struggling? How could we let anybody know that Dad had totally screwed up? Mom had stopped paying my allowance. I had to quit ballet and tennis lessons. When Jimmy outgrew his sneakers, Mom just sat down and cried. There was no way I could ask for new school clothes when the ones from last year were technically fine.

And I couldn't have anybody over to the duplex—the place was horrible. The family next door was horrible. They had a big loud dog tied to a post in the front yard, and a painted plaster gnome the size of Jimmy on their porch. Every now and then the dog lifted his leg and peed on the gnome. It was a totally disgusting place to live. When we moved there, everyone assumed that it was temporary, that we were simply looking for a smaller house to buy. That's the impression Mom gave people—and maybe she believed it herself. Maybe she believed everything would work out in a month or two. Instead we ended up in a place that made the duplex look good. The Golden Crown Inn. That was a week from hell—I couldn't even think about it without feeling sick.

When I transferred to Randolf, I didn't make an effort to meet people—what was the point? People would say hi in class, but that was it. And that's the way I wanted it. I ate lunch in the art room, where no one would bother me. Not that I was the only one who ate in there. Ms. Ashland, the art teacher, left the door open for students to come in and work. A group always gathered there, the kind of people Kari and Amanda called flower children when we saw them hanging out downtown or throwing Frisbees in the park. They weren't the kind of people who went to Bentley or the kind who would pay any attention to me, sitting on the other side of the art room with my peanut butter sandwich and my sketchbook.

It was weird, but before long I hardly missed my old friends. It's like what held us together wasn't each other. It was the stuff we used to do—the parties and shopping and Bentley activities. I missed the things we did; without

them there wasn't much between us. Maybe that was because I'd only gone to Bentley for a year.

Or maybe there just hadn't been much there to
begin with.

I reached the main entrance just as the first bell was ringing, and I slipped into first period with the second bell.
Mom had visited the school last week to explain things. I
guess she had to change the address and phone number
on my records again. Mr. Smith, my math teacher, looked
up as I came in but didn't say anything. He must know, I
thought. All my teachers must know where I was living
now. Just thinking about that made me feel sick. All
morning I had trouble concentrating. We were doing
quadratic equations in math, which I didn't understand at
all, and in social studies we were three chapters into a
unit on communism. I was behind in everything.

I should have spent lunch period asking my teachers
what I needed to do to catch up, but instead I went
straight to the art room and sat in the far corner, away
from the table where the flower children would be gathering with their tofu and guava juice. I pulled out my portfolio and looked over some of the drawings I'd done last
semester. What a bunch of junk. The portrait of Jimmy
looked like an old man. The duplex neighbor's noisy dog
looked like a pig. The still life I'd considered entering in
the student show was stiff and lacked perspective. The
one talent I thought I had—well, I'd been fooling myself.
Putting my portfolio away, I took my sketch pad and a
felt-tip pen out of my backpack and started messing
around. Before I knew it, I'd drawn a rhinoceros with a

long curved tusk and wrinkled eyes. A man with a mustache. A skeleton pushing a lawn mower.

"That's really good," someone said. I flipped the sketchbook shut. One of the flower children that I remembered from last semester, a guy with dreadlocks and an eyebrow piercing, was leaning over the table looking at my sketches.

"Sorry." He grinned and held up his hands. "Didn't mean to invade your space."

"No, it's okay," I said, feeling myself blush. "You just startled me." I hadn't meant to be rude, but I wasn't used to anyone coming up to me like that.

"You're in my art class this semester," he said. "Second period, right? I saw your stuff up at the fall semester show too. You're really good."

"Thanks," I said. People were always telling me that. But it didn't mean much. What's good in high school is nothing in the real art world. I hadn't even wanted to enter the show, but Ms. Ashland had talked me into it.

"I'm Aspen." He stuck out his hand like he was some kind of salesman.

"Like the tree?" I asked, then felt stupid.

"Like the town, actually. In Colorado. I was conceived there."

"I'm Lucy," I said, thinking that his conception wasn't really an appropriate topic of conversation, considering we'd just met.

"Yeah, I know." He grinned, then waved his arm toward the flower children sitting around the table in the opposite corner. A girl with a long black braid and green eyes was watching him. "Want to join us?"

"I've got to catch up on some assignments," I said. "But thanks."

"Anytime. We don't bite." He laughed. "We're mostly vegetarians."

From then on Aspen came over and talked to me for a couple of minutes every day after lunch. By the end of the week I kind of looked forward to seeing him. For one thing, I was starting to like the way he looked. He dressed like a street person and his hair was totally weird, but he had brown eyes so dark you couldn't see the pupils, and a great smile that started out slow, then spread across his face. Sometimes I'd catch myself watching him work during second period. He sat hunched over his drawing, his face still with concentration. He didn't talk to me in class. Ms. Ashland was very strict. The study of art was not for slackers, she said at least twice a day.

Sometimes I watched him as he ate lunch with the other hippies. He was always kidding around, always laughing. He might drape his arm around a girl for a few seconds or pull another one over to sit on his lap. There was something about him they all liked, but no one seemed to be with him. He was a flirt, I decided. And then I wondered why I cared. He wasn't my type. Not in the least. So I was surprised when he asked me what I was doing that weekend.

"I don't know yet," I said. *Nothing* was the real answer. Or more precisely, taking long walks by myself, doing homework, sleeping as much as possible.

"You want to do something? Maybe go to a movie?"

I was caught completely off guard. Here was this guy, a

complete flirt, with weird hair and a silver hoop circling his eyebrow, asking me out. I think. Amanda and Kari would have died laughing if they knew.

"I can't," I said. "I've got to take care of my brother."

"All weekend?" Aspen asked, his smile slowly spreading over his face.

"My mom's going out of town," I lied. "I'm really busy."

"Could I call you sometime?"

"I guess." I tried to sound calm, thinking, *We don't have a phone.* All calls went through the main office. In a panic I gave him my old number, the one from when I lived in a normal house like a normal person. Probably he wouldn't call anyhow.

"Okay." He wrote down the number on his wrist with my felt-tip pen, then touched the back of my hand. "Talk to you later."

As he walked out of the room, I wanted to call him back and say yes, I'd go out with him. For months nobody had invited me to do anything. For months I'd been thinking it didn't matter. My eyes started stinging. The still life I was working on blurred. I might have completely lost it if Ms. Ashland hadn't come into the room and commented on my work. I don't know what she said. I don't know if I even answered her.

How was I going to get through the rest of the day? I wondered. How was I going to get through the rest of my life?

4

When I got back to St. Agatha's, Jimmy was throwing a tantrum.

"I want to watch Woody and Buzz!" he shouted at Mom, and kicked a bucket of LEGOs across the room. Then he crawled into his blanket house and wouldn't come out.

"You need to stay with me tonight," Mom said as she gathered up the LEGOs. "We'll read books. We'll color." I could hear a slight edge of desperation in her voice.

"I don't want to stay with you. I want to watch Woody and Buzz!"

Friday night is kids' movie night at St. Agatha's. All week a sign had been posted on the bulletin board announcing *Toy Story 2*.

"But you don't know any of the other boys and girls." Mom tried to reason with him. "You wouldn't

29

like to stay down there with children you don't know, would you?"

"Let him go," I said. Mom looked at me as if I'd suggested putting him out on the street.

"I can't let him go down there by himself," she protested. Her hands were full of LEGOs.

"He won't be by himself. There are a dozen other kids. And the volunteers will be there," I said. "Don't you think he needs to meet some of the other boys?"

"The other boys here?" Mom asked. Where else is he going to make friends? I thought. "But they're so rough. Look at that little boy who fractured his arm last weekend."

"Alonzo fractured his own arm, not some other kid's," I said. "Jimmy's been cooped up in this room for most of the week. He needs a break, Mom. You need one too."

"But he's only five," she said. "And he's small for his age. And these other children, they're not the kind of children—"

"Look, I'll take him myself," I said before she could finish. "I'll hang out down there and make sure he's okay. If any of the other kids start acting up, I'll bring him right back upstairs."

"No, I'll go." Mom dropped the LEGOs into the bucket. "I'll sit with him."

"You need a break," I said. "Why don't you go somewhere by yourself?"

"Where would I go?" she asked.

"I don't know. Just go walk around the mall or something."

At least I had school to escape to. Mom had spent

30

most of her week inside St. Agatha's. Inside room 12, to be exact. On her trips out she'd gone to the grocery store, paying with the food stamps she hated to use but couldn't manage without. She'd spent some time in the library and signed up at a couple of temp agencies, even though she'd failed the typing tests. On Tuesday night she'd gone to a résumé-writing class and had come back depressed because she couldn't fill even half a page. On Wednesday she'd visited the lawyer only to discover that Dad's social security payment had been minimal. He'd underestimated his income, Mom said. But I understood. He'd cheated. The question of life insurance was still unanswered, and the IRS was sending her letters. She was definitely worried.

She had also visited Dad's grave.

When he'd first died, she'd gone to the cemetery every day, but now she drove out there only a couple of times a week. I'd gone with her and Jimmy Wednesday after school to remove the silk poinsettias that were fading at the foot of the huge granite headstone. How much had that thing cost? I wondered as I ran my hand over my father's name and dates. Then I was ashamed of myself for putting a price on his memorial.

Jimmy took my hand. "Is Daddy in there?"

"In where?"

"There." He pointed at the granite stone.

"No, Jimmy. He's underneath," I said. "I mean his body is. He's . . . somewhere else."

Jimmy looked around as if he expected Dad to sneak up and grab him like he used to do.

"Where? Where is he?"

"I don't know exactly. Somewhere good. Like heaven."

"Can he see us?"

How should I answer that? Would Jimmy want him to be able to see us or not? Jimmy always seemed a little afraid of Dad. Maybe because Dad had worked long hours and, when he was home, had spent most of his time watching sports on TV. Maybe because he'd been so big and kind of loud. Or maybe Jimmy could sense that Dad had been disappointed in having a son so small and quiet.

"Do you miss him?" I asked.

Jimmy frowned up at me. "I don't know. Do you?"

"Sure," I said. How could I say anything else? Dad deserved the headstone. He had deserved the nice funeral, the fine coffin, because he'd been a good father. Hadn't he given us everything we ever wanted? If only he'd been more careful, I thought, fighting the tears as Mom stuffed the tattered poinsettias into a plastic bag.

It took a while, but I finally convinced Mom to let me take Jimmy down to the playroom for movie night. The movie hadn't started yet, but a lot of kids were gathered there waiting. The volunteers were trying to get them to settle down. Carlos called to Jimmy as soon as we entered the room.

"Sit here with me and Lonzo!" Despite Mom's precautions, Jimmy had gotten to know some of the kids. Maybe because Mom was a little overprotective, Jimmy was a shy kid. But Carlos, like Jan, was very friendly, and he seemed to have taken Jimmy on as a special buddy. He and Alonzo made room for Jimmy in a big beanbag chair. They looked like some kind of culturally aware TV commercial, a chubby brown kid, a skinny black kid and Jimmy, the freckled white kid, all with great big grins on their faces. He'd be fine watching the movie without me. Even though I'd told Mom I'd stay with him, I planned to go to the library. I had my sketchbook and pastels and wanted some time alone.

"I'll be right down the hall," I told him. "Get one of the grown-ups if you need help finding me."

"Okay," he said absently. He was drawing a smiley face on Alonzo's cast.

"So, where will I be?" I asked, gently shaking his shoulder.

"Right down the hall. In the library," he said, and looked at me with steady gray eyes. "I can find my way around, Lucy. I'm not a baby, you know."

I knew. It was Mom who hadn't figured that out yet.

Fortunately, the library was empty. All four tables were cleared off, and the chairs were neatly arranged. I sat at the table farthest from the door, the one partly hidden by a narrow shelf of beat-up children's books, and opened my sketch pad. I'd just gotten into a picture of a man with wings when the door opened and Crystal came in. Slouching down in my chair and scooting a little farther behind the bookcase, I hoped she wouldn't notice me. She pulled a baby monitor, a kitchen timer and a thick math book from an orange plastic tote bag. Then she sat down and turned the volume up on the baby monitor.

Even from the other side of the room I could hear her baby's rapid breathing over the mild static. She set the timer and started on math problems. Either she hadn't seen me slumped behind the bookcase or she was doing a great job of ignoring me.

She leaned over her book and wrote with her left hand. Her two-tone hair was pushed behind her ears, and I could see her profile clearly. Her nose was straight and small, her chin and forehead both a little prominent, her lips full. Her eyelids were heavy and fringed with long black lashes. Occasionally I'd catch a glimpse of her pale blue eyes. Quietly I turned a page in my sketchbook and started drawing her.

For thirty minutes I sketched, and then the timer went off and she looked straight at me.

"In case you're wondering, I'm studying for my GED."

"I wasn't," I said. She'd known I was in the room all along.

"They have GED classes over at the community college, but I prefer to study alone."

"Okay . . ." I couldn't figure out why she was telling me this. Was she trying to impress me? With a GED?

"I set this timer for two reasons." She held the kitchen timer like she might pitch it at me. "One, so I stick to what I'm supposed to be doing, and two, so I don't have to wear a watch. I can't stand a watch." She put her ear to the baby monitor for a second. "What are you doing? Homework?"

"Just sketching." I closed the sketchbook and crossed my arms over it.

"Let me see." I reluctantly flipped opened the book

and showed her the man with wings. She didn't seem to pick up on the fact that I found her totally irritating.

"That can't be all you got done sitting there for thirty minutes."

I stared at her but didn't turn the page. What made her think I was interested in talking to her, much less showing her my work?

"I know you were drawing me," she said. Instead of getting offended, she smiled. When Crystal smiled, she became surprisingly pretty. Dimples appeared in her cheeks and her perfect teeth flashed between her lips. "Let me see it," she said. "Please?"

Maybe it was the please. I turned to her portrait. For a minute she looked at it carefully, then she said, "You got my nose too big, but that's pretty good. You can tell it's me, anyway. Let me see some more."

I turned to sketches of Jimmy, to the skeleton with the lawn mower, to the rhinoceros. To the man with the mustache.

"Who's that?" she asked.

"Someone I knew once."

"It's your father, isn't it."

I didn't answer.

"Jan told me about him. About the wreck. You go to Randolf?" she asked, changing the subject abruptly.

"This is my first year there."

"Where'd you go before?"

"Bentley Academy," I said.

"That snobby rich-kid school?" She made a prim face and sniffed pretentiously. "I thought you looked preppy. I used to go to Randolf, till I dropped out. I should have stayed, but like a dumbass I didn't. I'd be graduating this year. What year are you?"

"Sophomore," I said. I couldn't decide whether to be offended by what she said, or to laugh.

"My boyfriend's a senior there," she said. "So, doesn't your mama know anybody that can get y'all out of here? Where are her friends?"

"They're around," I said. The truth was that Mom didn't really have any. She was involved in a lot of organizations, she had a lot of acquaintances, but in the two years we'd lived in Cottonwood Falls, she hadn't become close to anyone. Because of Dad's business, we'd lived in a lot of places—Moses Lake, Yakima, Bellevue, Cottonwood Falls—all since I'd started school. Maybe it was just easier not to get close to people.

"You look like you ought to have some rich relatives somewhere," Crystal continued.

"I don't," I said, not that it was any of her business. "My grandparents are dead. My father was an only child. My mother has a sister, but I've never met her."

"Why not?"

"They're not close," I said vaguely. The only thing I knew about Mom's sister was that she was older than Mom and that her name was Kathy.

"You ought to get in touch with her. Rich people don't like to leave their relatives in places like this. It's not good for the family reputation."

"How do you know my aunt's rich?" I asked.

"By looking at you."

"Me?"

"And your mother," Crystal said. "You two look like

36

you just walked off a cruise ship. Blond as they come, moving like you own the world, dressed like that. And you went to Bentley Academy."

"What's that got to do with my aunt?"

"You and your mom come from money. So she comes from money. And money marries money. Go figure," Crystal said like she was some expert in social class. A small cry came over the baby monitor. "There's Chelsea Rose. I got to go." She shoveled her things into the plastic tote bag, hoisted it over her shoulder and hurried out of the room.

When the movie was over, Jimmy found me in the library. He wanted to know if Carlos and Alonzo could come over and play LEGOs. As if room 12 were our house, I thought. As if there would be space in there for those three.

"Not tonight, Jim," I said as his friends gazed up at me. "Maybe you could bring your LEGOs down here tomorrow."

"Mommy won't let me," he said. "She says they'll get lost."

"Maybe she'll change her mind. Tell the guys good night. It's past your bedtime."

"I don't have a bedtime," Alonzo said. "We got a TV in our room, and I can watch it anytime, all night even, long as I turn off the sound."

"Well, good for you," I said. "Jimmy's got to go to bed now."

"Bye, Mr. J-man," Carlos said, and he and Alonzo ran down the hall giggling.

" 'Mr. J-man'?" I asked.

"That's my name," Jimmy said. "Don't wear it out."

"How was the movie?" Mom asked before we even got through the door. She was sitting on the bed reading one of the magazines donated to St. Agatha's library, an old *House Beautiful* that someone had dropped off. Maybe as a bad joke.

"Good," Jimmy said. "Carlos and Alonzo were there."

Mom gave him a tense little smile. "Well, let's get you into some jammies and into bed."

"Why don't we have a TV in our room?" Jimmy asked as Mom pulled his shirt over his head. "Alonzo's mommy lets him watch TV all night long."

"I'll take him to brush his teeth," I said quickly. The less Mom knew about Alonzo's and Carlos's personal lives, the better.

After his bedtime story Jimmy snuggled under the down comforter Mom had brought from the old house, and fell right to sleep. I was tired too, but Crystal mentioning relatives who could help out had gotten me thinking. When we first moved to the duplex, I'd been convinced there must be someone who could help us. I'd mentioned my aunt Kathy, but Mom had refused to talk about it. I'd let it go at the time, thinking things would work out for us soon enough. But things had gone from bad to worse. Maybe it was time to try again.

"Did you ever tell Kathy that Dad died?" I asked, just as she was about to turn off the bedside lamp.

"Kathy?" she asked, her hand frozen in the air beside the lamp.

"Your sister. Don't you think she'd want to know?"

"I'm sure she's heard by now."

"You never wrote her?" I asked, trying to keep the conversation going. "Maybe she could help out, give us a loan or something."

"She wouldn't help us if her life depended on it," Mom said, and turned off the light.

"If you just got in touch with her . . . ," I persisted. "Whatever happened between you two can't be more important than this, can it?"

Mom turned the light back on. "Under no circumstances do I plan to get in touch with her. And under no circumstances will *you* try to get in touch with her." She shook her head. "Can't you just trust me?"

"Okay. Jeez. I was just asking," I said as she turned off the light again.

Did I trust her? I wondered as I lay in the dark. How could I, when St. Agatha's was the best option she could come up with?

5

Even though it was Saturday morning, I was up early. It was almost impossible to sleep, despite quiet hours. People were up all night, flushing toilets, opening and closing doors. Babies cried. By six a.m. kids were running up and down the halls. By six-thirty the showers were going. By seven I was down in the kitchen fixing Jimmy a bowl of instant oatmeal and wondering what I'd do with myself all day. We'd been at St. Agatha's for just over two weeks, but it seemed like forever. This time last year we were sitting down to one of Mom's pancake breakfasts. Drinking fresh-squeezed orange juice and hot chocolate before we took off for a day of skiing.

Carlos and Alonzo tumbled into the kitchen. I'd seen Alonzo's mother, Tina, only a couple of times. She was tall and very thin, and she hummed to herself constantly. Alonzo seemed to spend most of his time with Jan and

Carlos. When Jan came into the kitchen a minute later, she waved and stuck a couple of Pop-Tarts in the toaster. For a large woman she moved quickly, almost gracefully. She and Carlos would make a good subject for a drawing, I thought, if I could get them to sit still long enough.

"Looks like more snowy weather," Jan said as she sat Carlos and Alonzo down at the table. "After breakfast I'm taking the boys sledding. You think Jimmy'd want to go?"

"Yeah, J-man, go with us," Carlos said.

Jimmy started bouncing in his seat. "Can I go? Can I?"

"Maybe," I said, although I knew there was no way Mom would let him leave St. Agatha's with Jan. "If I go too, maybe he can go," I told Jan.

"There's a good hill down at Regal Park. I'll ask Rachel if we can take a couple of sleds." Jan poured the boys apple juice. "If we leave right after breakfast, we'll beat the crowds. With this new snow the whole neighborhood will be there by ten o'clock."

By eight-thirty the boys were sailing down the hill at Regal Park on bright green plastic sleds. I was surprised at Jimmy, who raced down the hill without a second's hesitation. In the short time we had been at St. Agatha's, he'd changed from an overgrown toddler to a real kid.

"What's your mama doing this morning?" Jan asked. We stood in the violet shadows of some pine trees, out of the way of the sleds.

"When we left, she was getting dressed," I said. "I don't know what she's got planned."

"She don't like it here much, does she?"

"She hates it," I said. "But she'd never tell anybody that. She's too polite."

"What about you?"

"I'll tell anybody, I'd rather be anywhere else, almost."

"Remember the *almost*. There's a lot of places worse than St. Agatha's," Jan said.

"Yeah, I know." I remembered the motel we'd stayed in over Christmas, the police breaking into the room next door. I knew that some of St. Agatha's residents had come right off the streets. I thought about Jan and her meth house. "But I don't know how we're going to get out of here unless Mom can find a job."

Mom had decided she could get her associate's degree in administrative office systems, which had something to do with computers and business, as far as I could tell, and paid well. She'd start classes next week. A few of the courses she'd taken at Washington State University almost twenty years ago would transfer as general credits. If she took a full load every quarter, she'd be finished in a year. But a year was too long. We needed to get out sooner than that.

If I could get a job next summer, and if she could work part-time and get some student loans, I figured we could maybe be out by the time school started again in September.

Or if I contacted my aunt. She and Mom already weren't talking to each other. The worst she could do was say no. But what woman, no matter how unsympathetic she might be, would let her sister stay in a homeless shelter?

"Do you have any siblings?" I asked Jan.

"Seven," she answered. "I've got a twin in Montana."

"Do you stay in touch?"

"Roberta, my twin, calls every Sunday night."

"What about the others?"

"Nah, most of them don't even claim me," Jan said.

"Why not?"

Jan screwed her mouth to one side. "About as many reasons as there are siblings, I guess. Religion in one case. Money in another. The fact I was using in almost all cases."

"Using?" I asked.

"Drugs," Jan said. "I don't know who made up the lie that brothers and sisters are supposed to like each other. You didn't choose them, they didn't choose you. It's like poker: You take what you're dealt. So what are the odds you'll get a winning hand?"

Maybe Mom and her sister just didn't like each other. And if that was the only problem, couldn't they put their issues aside and deal with finding us a place to live?

"My feet are about to freeze off," Jan said suddenly. "You ready to go?"

Now that Jan mentioned it, I was having trouble feeling my toes. We let the boys take one more ride down the hill, then we trudged back to St. Agatha's.

"I'm going to stir up a pot of hot chocolate. Want some?" Jan asked as we came in the door. I pulled off Jimmy's wet gloves and held his cold red hands in mine until he jerked away and ran after Carlos.

"Sure, that sounds good."

"Why don't you go get your mama?" Jan said. "It's not good to stay off by yourself like that all the time."

"My mama stays off by herself," Alonzo said, pulling his knit cap down over his eyes.

"Yeah, you're right as usual, Lonzo," Jan said, then turned to me and spoke in a low voice. "His mama's on about ten different meds. She's better off by herself, bless her heart."

I didn't think Mom would join us, but she did. She was still uncomfortable and reserved with the other residents. But who could blame her? Living with dropouts and re-formed addicts and women who had to report to CPS. My mother might be homeless, but she was none of the above. She had attended only one of the "recommended" classes so far, and she'd only gone because Paula had urged her to participate. Whether she really did partici-pate or not, I don't know. She was diligent about her cleaning responsibilities and cooperated with the rest of the crew, but she didn't mix well, and the other women knew it. Only Jan didn't seem to have a problem with Mom's attitude. She treated her like she treated everyone else. She shared whatever she was eating with her, and re-vealed more about herself than Mom needed or wanted to know. That morning Mom seemed to truly appreciate Jan's reaching out to her. They sipped hot chocolate from heavy mugs and talked about going back to school and about their kids.

While we were drinking our second cup of hot chocolate, Crystal came in with her baby on her hip. Jan poured her a mug of cocoa, and she sat down next to me, across from

Mom, and listened to Carlos tell her about the sledding adventure.

"Next time we'll take Chelsea Rose," he said. The baby smiled when she heard her name.

"Chelsea Rose is too little right now, but next winter maybe she can ride a sled," Crystal said. She turned to Jan. "You think I could put some of that hot chocolate in her bottle once it cools? I'm trying to wean her. Maybe chocolate will help."

"Don't see why not, right, Cindy?" Jan said. Mom pressed her lips together. She clearly had a different opinion about giving chocolate milk to a six-month-old, but at least she was keeping her mouth shut.

"I put almost everything in Carlos's baby bottle," Jan continued. "Milk, juice, Coke. His son-of-a-bitch father even filled it up with beer once." Mom's eyes widened. "That was only once, though. Pretty soon after that CPS took Carlos. That was the first time. When I got him back, his daddy was long gone, and good riddance."

Jan launched into a story about how her ex-husband took everything she owned when he left, including the turquoise jewelry she'd inherited from her Nez Perce grandmother. I gathered this ex-husband, Carlos's father, wasn't the same as the so-called boyfriend who had had the meth lab in the basement. Or the guy who worked at a chop shop in Idaho. Jan's life was so full of people it was hard to keep up with them all. And most of them you hoped never to meet.

Crystal shifted Chelsea Rose on her lap and fed her warm cocoa from the bottle. Chelsea Rose made snuffling noises, like a happy piglet. Surprisingly, Mom was absorbed in Jan's story, not just listening politely, and she looked more awake than she had in days.

"Shit, what time is it?" Crystal interrupted. Mom primly glanced at her watch and told her it was ten-twenty.

"Elton's picking me up in ten minutes to go to the mall. I got to put on some makeup." Crystal popped the bottle out of Chelsea Rose's surprised little mouth and grabbed her orange tote bag.

"Who is Elton?" I asked Jan as Crystal dashed out of the kitchen.

"Chelsea Rose's daddy. He's a nice boy, but he still lives with his parents, and they can't stand Crystal."

"He has visitation rights?" Mom asked.

"Oh, sure. Him and Crystal are planning to get married as soon as he finishes high school and gets a full-time job. Right now he works part-time and plays in a rock-and-roll band. They're not stupid enough to run off together yet. His parents would disown him, and then where would they be?"

Mom shook her head like these lives being lived around her were more than she could comprehend.

The rest of the day dragged. I got way ahead in *Great Expectations*, which we were reading in English, and took a walk. Then I went through my clothes and decided I hated everything I owned. I'd have given almost anything for a half hour at Macy's and unlimited funds. After dinner I messed around with some oil pastels. I sketched a face, gave it dreadlocks and warm brown eyes. Of course it was Aspen, and I found myself imagining what my weekend would have been like if I'd said yes. I could have gotten his number and called him. But the last thing I needed was to get involved with someone—especially a flirt, the darling of the hippie chicks. Someone Mom would never approve of.

The next afternoon I went down to the clothing room. I'd seen a woman in a Mercedes SUV drop off several large Nordstrom bags the day before, and I wanted to see what she'd left. Three weeks ago I wouldn't have believed I'd be going through someone's hand-me-downs, but I hadn't gotten anything new to wear since last summer. My sweaters had started to pill. My jeans were worn at the hems. I was sick of my wardrobe. And I was bored. This was as close to shopping as I was going to get for a while. I wasn't a clothes addict like Kari, who had stuff in her closet with the tags still attached, but I liked nice things. When I'd complained about my ratty jeans, Mom had suggested Target, a total conversation stopper. I was curious to see what the Mercedes lady had left. Most of the clothes were too professional-looking—Ralph Lauren suits, Jones New York trousers, old-lady pumps. But there were a couple of sweaters I liked, a black angora boatneck and a red turtleneck that looked like they'd never been worn. I tucked them under my arm and continued through the racks.

"Finding anything?" Crystal asked. She was leaning against the door with her arms crossed, and I suddenly felt both ashamed and protective of the sweaters.

"A couple of things," I said.

"You really have to look hard. Most of this is shit. But I'm good at finding stuff." The baby monitor crackled in her hand. She pulled a green sweater off the rack and held it up to her chest. "How's this?"

"Kind of bright for your complexion," I said, wondering why she cared about my opinion, why I bothered to give it.

"How's this blue one?"

"Better," I said.

She took off her shirt right in front of me and tried the sweater on.

"Looks good with your eyes," I said. I didn't want her to think I was giving her compliments, but it did look good on her.

"It's not too tight? My boobs got humongous after Chelsea Rose was born."

"You can get away with it." Crystal had a really nice shape. I hadn't noticed it before.

We rummaged through the clothes silently for a while, then Crystal said, "So did you ask your mom about her sister?"

"I mentioned it," I said warily. Why was Crystal so interested in my family? I knew she wasn't just making polite conversation. Polite wasn't her style. What was in it for her?

"And?"

"She didn't think it was a good idea to call. She . . ." She what? Said I should trust her to make decisions. Said I didn't know what I was talking about.

"You ever Google her?" Crystal asked.

"You mean on the Internet?"

"Of course on the Internet. Didn't you have computers at Bentley?" Crystal asked sarcastically. "What's her last name?"

"I don't know," I said, feeling both anxious and excited. What would Mom do if I did find Kathy? What if I contacted her and she wanted to help?

"You know her maiden name?" Crystal asked, interrupting the possibilities I was building in my head.

"Sinclair," I said. "Same as Mom's. Why do you want to know?"

"So I can find her."

"Why would you do that?"

"Something to do." She shrugged. "In case you haven't noticed, it gets pretty boring around here."

"You just search random people on the Internet for fun?" It sounded weird to me, even kind of creepy. "So, what if you find her?"

"If I find your aunt, you babysit Chelsea. I need somebody for Wednesday night."

"And if you don't find her?"

"I guess I'll have to stay home. Or ask Jan. We trade off. Chelsea Rose for Carlos, and usually that means Alonzo too."

"That doesn't sound fair."

"Nothing's ever fair," she said. "So is it a deal?"

"I guess," I said. She could try if she wanted, but I doubted she'd find anything.

6

Monday afternoon I came out of my sixth-period class and walked down Randolf's mostly empty halls. Every afternoon I hung around in the classroom for ten or fifteen minutes after the final bell. Mr. Phillips, my sixth-period science teacher, coached basketball, and he was out the door with the students. Nobody noticed me sitting there in the back copying down the homework assignment as slowly as I could. Most afternoons the whole school had cleared out by the time I came down the front steps.

But today Aspen was waiting for me. He was by himself, which was unusual. Most of the time he and his friends traveled in a flock. But there he stood, his hands in the pockets of his coat, his dreadlocks dancing in the strong breeze.

"Hey," he said, and grinned at me.

"Hi." I stood a couple of steps above him, wondering what he wanted.

"You waiting for a ride?" he asked.

"I walk."

"Then I'll walk with you. This way, right?" He pointed west, my usual route.

I shrugged and started down the sidewalk.

"How's your self-portrait going in art?" he asked.

"It's okay. It could be better."

"Nah, yours is the best in the class. You're really good."

"Thanks," I said. I was never satisfied with my work. What I envisioned in my head never came out that way on paper, and I didn't really want to talk about it.

"I tried to call you this weekend," he said.

"I guess I was out." I looked at the ground, watched my feet moving along the sidewalk.

"No. The number you gave me is no longer in service."

"Maybe you dialed it wrong. Or maybe you copied it down wrong."

"Maybe," he said. We walked in silence for a few minutes.

"Do you live around here?" I asked.

"I live over on Maple."

"But that's in the other direction," I said. "Why are you walking this way?"

"Maybe I just wanted to walk with you, and talk to you," he said. "Is that okay?"

"I guess." Although there were all kinds of subjects I couldn't touch, I was glad to have someone to talk to, to have someone, particularly a guy I might have considered liking under other circumstances, pay attention to me.

Luckily none of the untouchable subjects came up. Instead we talked about music and *Great Expectations*, which he'd read last year in sophomore English, and the new tardy policy, which we both agreed sucked.

All of a sudden Aspen stopped and pointed at a large formation of geese flying overhead. "Migrating," he said. We watched them move out of sight, their calls fading as they faded against the gray sky.

"They are so great," Aspen said softly. "Did you hear them calling to each other? Like they're checking up to make sure everyone's okay."

I nodded. "Sometimes I wish I were a bird," I said, and then felt like an idiot.

"Yeah, I know what you mean," Aspen said, taking me completely seriously. "Free, right? Independent. If you were a bird, what kind would you be?"

"I bet you ask all the girls you meet that question," I said.

Aspen laughed. "No, really. What would you be?"

"I don't know. I never thought about it. How about you?"

"A crow," he said. "They're really intelligent."

"Smarter than owls?"

"Owls just look smart. Crows know how to use tools. And steal things."

"Smarter than parrots?"

He laughed. "Who'd want to be a parrot?"

"Okay. If I were a bird, I think I'd be a hawk. I like how they move," I said.

"I can see you as a hawk," he said. "A sparrow hawk, quick and graceful. Circling the sky alone, always watching the world around you." He put his arms out and zigzagged along the sidewalk. "And hawks don't have a song."

"What makes you think I don't have a song?" I asked, pleasantly embarrassed that he'd described me as graceful, but wondering about the song comment.

"I don't know, I just guessed," he said. "And you don't, do you? Not right now."

I shrugged. "I never thought about it before."

We got to the corner where I turned toward St. Agatha's, and I said I had to go.

"You're not going to let me walk you all the way?" he asked in a teasing voice. "Do you have an evil stepmother who chases away your friends?"

I stumbled around for an answer, but Aspen laughed lightly.

"Hey, just kidding." He gave my arm a quick squeeze. "See you tomorrow?"

"Okay," I said. "And thanks."

"For what?" he asked.

"For walking with me. And talking."

"Anytime," he said, already heading back in the direction we had come.

Anytime. Maybe in a perfect world. But right now I couldn't have him walking me home. He'd find out where I lived, and that would be the end of that. Nobody wanted to go out with a homeless person. Still, I could see him at school. We could talk there, couldn't we? I could look into his warm eyes and pretend we were friends.

· · ·

When I got back, I could hear Jimmy screaming before I even opened the door. He was crumpled on the floor. Mom held both of his wrists, trying to make him stand up.

"I want to go to the mall with Lonzo and Carlos!" he shouted.

"I've told you no, and that's final," Mom said between clenched teeth. "Now stand up!"

The warm glow I'd held tightly all the way from the corner, the glow of Aspen's laugh, turned cold and disappeared as Mom managed to jerk Jimmy off the floor and spank his behind. The smack glanced off the seat of his blue jeans and couldn't have hurt, but both Jimmy and Mom froze for a second before Jimmy let out a shriek. I'd never seen Mom hit him before, not even a gentle swat. She looked horrified at what she'd done.

"It's okay," I said. "It didn't hurt him. He's being a brat."

"But I hit him," she said.

"Jimmy, be quiet!" I said, and he fell onto the bed, his face muffled in the pillows. "What's going on, anyway?" I asked, trying to stay calm.

"Jan invited him to go with the boys to play video games at the mall. You know we don't have money to throw away like that," Mom said. "And besides, I can't just let him *go*."

"Maybe he needs to get out for a little while," I said. "Maybe it's worth five dollars to give him a change of scenery."

"He's not going anywhere now, not after that display," she said. Then she slumped into the chair. "What's happening to us?"

I knelt down beside her and put my hand on her shoulder.

"Nothing's happening. We're still us," I said. "We'll be out of here soon, and then everything will be okay."

"Ever since your father died, it's like I've got no control over anything." I rubbed her back. "It's like I'm becoming one of them."

"One of who?"

"The women here! Women who have their kids taken away."

"You aren't like that!" I said. "You're doing the best you can."

I went to the bed and lay down next to Jimmy. "You want to go make a snow house?" I whispered in his ear. He didn't say anything. His little body was pressed stiffly into the mattress.

"You and I can make an igloo in the courtyard while Mom cooks dinner." He shook his head into the pillow. "Oh, come on. I've been in school all day just thinking about it."

Jimmy sat up and looked over at Mom. She was facing the window. In the late afternoon light I could see a tear slide down her face. He rolled off the bed and crawled up in her lap. "Me and Lucy are going to make an igloo. That's a snow house," he explained carefully. "Want to come?"

Mom wiped her cheek and smiled. "Not today. You go and make a house, and in a little while we'll have dinner."

"Get your boots on," I said, then turned to Mom. "You okay?"

"I'm just stressed out about school, I guess," Mom said. "I haven't sat in a classroom in twenty years."

"You'll do fine," I said.

"I feel like I'm back in high school," she said. "I just hope I can do this."

"You can." I pulled Jimmy's hat down over his ears.

"And Jimmy will be going to preschool." Her voice faded off.

"He'll love preschool, won't you, Jimmy?" I said, smiling at him.

"But he's never been all day before," Mom said. "And at the Y." Even though Dad had disagreed, Mom had insisted that she could homeschool Jimmy until first grade. He was too small, too shy, she said. As a compromise he'd gone to a morning program two days a week at the Methodist church. Going all day to the YMCA program for low-income families would be totally different.

Jimmy and I were building the walls of the snow house when Crystal came out into the courtyard. She had Chelsea Rose bundled so tightly into a pink snowsuit she could hardly move.

"Nice work," she said to Jimmy as he proudly showed her the igloo. She put her hand on his head and twisted his cap around, making him laugh; then she turned to me. "I got something for you," she said, and pulled a piece of paper out of her pocket. It was a printout from the *Seattle Times* online.

KATHERINE SINCLAIR HALPERIN was named Volunteer of the Year by the Seattle Arts Council for her tireless efforts with the Seattle

Symphony and the Ballet and
Bubbly New Year's fund-raiser. Mrs.
Halperin graduated with a degree
in art history from the University
of Washington. She is the wife
of Wilson S. Halperin of Stokes,
Halperin and Anders, Attorneys
at Law.

Along with the article was a picture of a woman who
looked a lot like my mother, only blonder, sleeker and
better dressed.

"She looks like Cindy, doesn't she?" Crystal asked.
"You think that's her?"

"It could be." I studied the photo. Could it really be
her? She had the right name and looked about the right
age. And there was no denying the resemblance. "So
what am I supposed to do with this information?"

"That's up to you." She put her hand to Chelsea Rose's
red cheeks. "It's getting too cold out here, I got to take her
in. What are you doing tonight?"

"Homework."

"Meet me down in the computer room after dinner."

Dinner that night was especially chaotic, with two
middle-school-age girls getting into a catfight. Mom
whisked Jimmy out of his chair and out of the room as
their mothers, yelling obscenities at each other, pulled
the girls apart. Rachel took the girls and their mothers
into her office and shut the door.

"Ten to one they're fighting over some snot-nosed

little boy," Jan said as she sat down next to me. "It's always boys that make girls act like that. They'll share everything from bras to jelly beans, but let a boy come into the picture and the girls just go crazy."

"Their mothers weren't behaving much better," I said.

"Those two never could get along. If it isn't one of them coming to talk to me about the other, it's the other coming to talk about the one."

"Have they been here long?"

"Ruthanne, seven months. She's got her head on straight most of the time. But her in the black skirt? She's always stirring things up. Thank god she's moving out soon."

"This place will make you crazy," I said.

"Or sane," Jan said. "Depends on what shape you're in when you get here, I guess. Without St. Agatha's I'd be in jail. Or dead."

"What about Tina?" I said, nodding at Alonzo's mother. She was playing with one of the toasters. "Is it making her crazy or sane?"

"I don't think St. Agatha's has anything to do with what shape Tina's in," Jan said, shaking her head. "Some days she's okay, some days she's not."

"This is one of her not days?" I asked.

"Yeah. I don't know if she's getting worse or just coming out of her room more," Jan said. Tina looked up as Jan approached her.

"They need to fix these things," Tina said.

"You want a Pop-Tart?" Jan asked, and stuck one in the toaster. "You go on over there and get yourself a seat."

Tina seemed to calm down as Jan spoke. I was

beginning to see that Jan had a way with people, a way of reaching them. She'd done the same thing with me that first morning, with Mom that morning after the sledding. Everybody at St. Agatha's seemed to respect her, even to depend on her. Given all she'd been through, it was pretty amazing.

After I cleaned up our dinner dishes, I went down to the computer room. Crystal was already there. She'd gotten into the Seattle phone directory and found the listing for Wilson Halperin. My uncle, I thought, and felt kind of weird. There was a phone number but no street address.

"What am I supposed to do now?" I asked. "Just give her a call?"

Crystal shook her head. "Her husband's a lawyer. They probably screen their calls. What you need to do is get in touch with her directly."

"That is, if I decide to get in touch at all."

"You do what you want," Crystal said. "Alls I'm doing is finding information."

"And getting a babysitter."

"That too. I'll need you from six-thirty till ten-thirty tomorrow."

"Four hours!"

"Hey, she'll be asleep most of the time. You got something better to do?"

"No," I admitted, and looked back at the screen. "Say I did want to get in touch with her. How am I supposed to find the address?"

"One step at a time," Crystal said, tapping her teeth with her fingernail. "Let me think about it."

"So how'd you learn to do all this investigation stuff?" I asked.

"I just picked it up. Anybody could do it."

"And you're teaching yourself algebra."

"Hey, rich girl." Crystal narrowed her blue eyes. "I may be homeless, but I'm not stupid."

"That's not what I meant," I said. Crystal always seemed to want an argument, and I seemed to be an easy target.

"Relax," she said. "I'm just giving you shit. But it's true, isn't it? Most people who have money think poor people are dumbasses." She shook her head. "Up through seventh grade I had all As. In eighth grade I barely passed, but it wasn't because I all of a sudden got stupid."

"What happened?"

"Screwed up my priorities. At least that's what the social worker said. I got an older boyfriend and started partying and smoking too much weed. The social workers thought it had to do with my mother going to jail and me having to live with my grandmother."

"Didn't your grandmother do anything about it?"

"Like what?"

"I don't know, ground you or something?"

Crystal laughed. "Ground me? Half the time she was the one I got weed from, her or one of her boyfriends. Besides, grounding me would have meant I'd be at home. She was much happier when she didn't know where I was."

"What about your mother?"

"Fifteen years for assorted felonies. She may get time off for good behavior, but I doubt it."

I was going to ask Crystal about her father, when Mom opened the door. Crystal quickly closed the computer screen.

"I thought I'd find you here. Working on homework?" Mom asked, glancing at the screen.

"Just doing a little research, but we're finished," I said. "At least for now."

7

The next morning Mom offered to drive me to Randolf before her first class, but I told her no. She was a nervous wreck. She kept checking her bag to make sure her registration stuff was in there. Plus she was still anxious about putting Jimmy in preschool. She didn't need to worry about me as well. Besides, no matter how heavily the snow was falling, I liked my walk to school. It was the only time during the whole day I had time to think. At school and the shelter I felt crowded and distracted, detached from what was going on around me. Maybe Aspen was right. Maybe I was like a hawk, aware of everything around me, but not really involved.

"Have a great first day!" I said to Jimmy as I slung my backpack over my shoulder. "You too, Mom." I kissed her cheek and headed out the door.

• • •

The snowflakes were blowing diagonally. Trees and buildings blurred grayish; nothing was clearly defined. The trackless sidewalk was covered with new snow, and only one other person, a tall guy leaning against a telephone pole, was out in this weather. It wasn't until I was a few feet from him that I realized the person was Aspen.

"What are you doing here?" I stopped, shocked to see him.

"I thought maybe we . . . maybe I could buy you a latte or something before school."

"How did you know?" I was embarrassed, angry that he'd found me.

He shrugged. "I followed you yesterday."

"You were *spying* on me? You were *stalking* me?"

"You can call it that if you want to, I guess."

"What would *you* call it?" I said, hurrying past him.

"Curiosity," he said. He put his hand on my arm. "Concern."

"I don't need your concern." I jerked my arm away and walked quickly through the blowing snow.

"Hey, I don't care where you live." He caught up with me. "Look, I'm sorry. I should have respected your privacy."

I stopped and turned back toward him. "I just didn't want anybody to find out."

"It's nothing to be ashamed of, Lucy. But I won't tell anybody if you don't want me to."

"But I didn't want *you* to find out either. Especially you." All of a sudden I was crying. I couldn't help it. Ever since we'd moved to St. Agatha's I had tried desperately not to get upset about things. Not to get angry about the night noises, about the lack of privacy and computer space and hot water. About feeling so helpless. I wouldn't let myself cry. What would be the point? But here I was in the middle of a snowstorm making a fool out of myself in front of the only person who mattered.

Without saying a word, Aspen put his arms around me, and I pressed my face against his chest. The zipper of his jacket felt cold against my cheek for a moment; then I felt warm all over and very, very tired. He took a tissue out of his pocket and handed it to me. I blew my nose and we started walking silently toward school.

"Meet me for lunch," he said when we got to the front steps of Randolf.

"Where, in the art room?"

"No, let's go down to the pizza place on Third. Ever eaten there?"

I shook my head.

"You'll like it." He took both my hands in his.

"Okay," I said.

"You're not mad?"

I shook my head again. "Somebody would have found out sooner or later. I'm glad it was you."

In second period Aspen caught my eye and winked. I winked back and turned to my self-portrait. The painting wasn't as bad as I remembered. It had potential. With a little more ochre in the hair and some shading under the chin, it was going to turn out okay.

At lunch we walked the two blocks to Michelangelo's Pizza. Aspen insisted on buying me a slice of vegetarian pizza and an Italian soda.

"Only if you let me pay you back someday," I said. "I'm a little short on cash lately." Just being able to say it, to almost joke about it, was a relief. One day I really would be able to pay him back. Soon, I hoped.

"You can draw a picture of my dog as a trade-off," he said, then told me about his West Highland terrier, Robert Burns, Bobby for short. During lunch Aspen never asked me a single question about my personal life. Still, I found myself telling him about Dad's accident, about moving into the duplex and changing schools, about living in the motel until we were placed at St. Agatha's.

"You've got a lot going on." He reached across the table and squeezed my hand. "And you still make it to school every day."

"If you lived with fifty other people, you'd be glad to go to school," I said.

That afternoon as he walked me home, I told him about St. Agatha's, about Crystal and Jan, Carlos and Alonzo, about no privacy, no room, no phone.

"I thought you gave me that fake number because you didn't want me to call you," he said. "I almost gave up."

"I'm glad you didn't," I said. "Thanks for stalking me."

He grinned. "Just for the record, I've never stalked anybody before."

"There's a first time for everything," I said, and gave him a quick hug. It felt like the right thing to do.

Wednesday was Food Bank Day at St. Agatha's, and that meant that regular donors, including the bakery two blocks away and several grocery stores, dropped off food. Usually the selection was pretty random. The bakery always sent loaves of white bread, but occasionally day-old cakes and donuts and éclairs would show up too. The grocery stores sent dented cans and whatever they had too much of—vegetables, milk, eggs. Other people would drop off boxes of cookies, macaroni and cheese, Korn Krisps. As on every other Wednesday, the kitchen was packed with women scrounging meals. Mom and Crystal were sorting through boxes while Jimmy entertained Chelsea Rose by making faces at her.

"What's this?" Crystal held up a piece of fruit for my mother to inspect.

"That's a mango," Mom said. "Lots of vitamins. You could mash some of that up and give it to Chelsea Rose, maybe put a little maple syrup on it."

"And these furry things?"

"Kiwis." Mom cut one into fourths and gave us each a slice. "They make amazing chutney, right, Lucy?" she said.

"Wonderful," I agreed, and bit into the tart green fruit. "How was school?"

"Overwhelming. But it's just the first day, nothing much happened." She was sorting through a bag of battered zucchini.

"Got any homework?" I asked, feeling like the parent.

"A little. I'll get to it after dinner." She had gathered a bag of vegetables and three cans of tomatoes. "How does vegetable lasagna sound?"

"Are you kidding? It sounds great!" I said. Mom hadn't made anything more interesting than meat loaf since we'd moved to St. Agatha's. Our old house in Andover

Hills had a huge kitchen with two ovens, granite counter-tops, an island with an extra sink. Dad had given Mom a complete set of Wolfgang Puck's signature cookware for her birthday. Now those pots and pans were in storage.

"Crystal, would you and Chelsea Rose like to have dinner with us?" Mom asked, completely surprising me.

"Sure," Crystal said, her mouth full of kiwi. "It'll beat frozen potpies."

"Maybe Jan and the boys would like to join us as well," Mom said. Now that she was back in the kitchen planning a dinner party—of sorts—she seemed almost happy.

When Jan offered to help, Mom sent her away. "But if you could keep an eye on Jimmy, that would be wonderful. Lucy can help me with the salad. If I can find some olive oil, I'll whip up some dressing." She wore one of her striped chef's aprons and was stirring the canned tomatoes into a thick sauce.

Right before the lasagna was ready, Mom found a white tablecloth. If we'd still been in Andover Hills, she would have lit candles and opened a bottle of wine, but neither wine nor candles were allowed at St. Agatha's. Still, the table looked pretty good. Even Carlos and Alonzo seemed subdued by the atmosphere Mom had managed to create.

"Your mom used to cook like this every night?" Crystal whispered.

"Pretty much," I said. Before Dad died, Mom had spent hours every day planning and preparing meals. She shopped for special ingredients, read cookbooks like other people read novels, and subscribed to *Gourmet* and *Food*

& Wine. She watched the Food Network. Every night there were flowers and candles on the table. I had never considered the time and money that went into her dinners. I had never considered that cooking was what my mother did. Which struck me for the first time as sad. Her world had been her kitchen. Now she was like some refugee trying to make the best of things. But at least she was trying.

"This is *good*," Jan said. "I never found anything like this in the Food Bank."

"It's less about the ingredients than what you do with them," Mom said. "Normally I would have used fresh mushrooms and shallots, but you make do with what you have."

After dinner Jan and Crystal insisted on cleaning up. I did my homework, then helped Mom with some math.

"I don't think I'll ever be able to understand this," she said, erasing half a page of calculations.

"Sure you can. Look at Crystal. She studies every day, even on Saturdays. Look at Jan, almost certified in education. If they can do this, so can you."

All that week I helped Mom with her homework. Math problems that seemed pretty simple to me were impossible for her. Even when she got the basic concept, she would make careless errors and come up with the wrong answer. By Friday she'd almost given up.

"One week down and nine to go," I told her. "It will get easier. You'll see."

Mom wasn't a housewife anymore. She wasn't living in a gated subdivision. She was a single parent who needed to pull her family out of the shelter and into a normal life. She didn't have the luxury of giving up. I had to make sure she didn't.

That night after Mom and Jimmy had fallen asleep, I got up and opened my sketchbook. In the light that shone through the window from the parking lot, I drew a woman in a 1950s-style dress and high heels. She wore a frilly apron and held a large bowl. When I finished, the picture looked like a vintage ad for cake mix. Except that where the woman's face should be was the number twelve.

8

Even though time moved slowly at St. Agatha's, January slipped away, and February was almost half over. Suddenly I was looking at my sixteenth birthday. The seven months since Dad's death had been so strange, I could hardly believe I had lived them.

The morning of my birthday I woke up early, before the showers came on, before kids started running up and down the halls. Not even a baby was crying. In the eerie silence I slipped out of bed and put on my bathrobe. It was cold and dark as I made my way downstairs to the empty living room. I looked out onto the courtyard, onto the snow lit yellow in the streetlight, and the bare trees and shrubs. February 13. Today started a new year of my life. Today I was sixteen.

If Dad hadn't died, Mom would be getting ready for my party. She'd be decorating a huge sheet cake with my name on it. I'd have my hair done, and my friends would bring me presents. And maybe there would be a new car parked outside after everybody sang "Happy Birthday." And Dad would hand me the keys and hug me while somebody caught it all on camera. *Happy birthday, honey.*

"I miss you," I said, and my breath clouded the windowpane. I hadn't missed him this much since he'd died. Not even at Christmas. Maybe the shock of losing so much had kept me from thinking about him. Now, after seven months, the reality of his absence felt almost like a physical presence. The presence of something solid and heavy and cold.

Lost in my thoughts of Dad and how everything had changed, I didn't hear Tina come into the room.

"You watching for him?" she asked quietly as she came up beside me. I stepped away from her as if by instinct.

"Watching for who?" I asked. I'd never really talked to Tina before. I realized now that I was a little afraid of her.

"The man," Tina said darkly. She gazed into the courtyard.

"What man?" I looked out the window.

"The one who comes at night and takes them away." I was about to ask what she meant, then realized the man existed only in her mind.

"You want to talk to Paula?" I asked.

Tina seemed to have forgotten about me. She scanned the courtyard in silence as I knocked on the door of the staff apartment.

"Paula," I called softly, my face against the door. "It's Lucy."

Paula opened the door. She had on her robe and slippers, but she looked ready for anything. "What's up?"

"Tina's acting kind of odd." I pointed toward the window where Tina stood talking to herself.

Paula squeezed my shoulder. "Thanks, I'll take care of her."

I watched as she led Tina to a couch and sat down with her. Maybe Tina was sleepwalking, I thought as I went back upstairs. Maybe some man really was after Alonzo—his father, a CPS worker. But I suspected the man Tina looked for out the window was only part of her bad dreams.

Mom sat up in bed when I opened the door to our room. "Are you all right?"

"I'm fine. I just had to use the bathroom," I whispered, not wanting to mention Tina.

"What time is it?" she asked, and Jimmy stirred beside her.

"Six o'clock. It's Saturday, you should go back to sleep."

"I don't think I could." She pulled on her robe.

I sat on the edge of my bed, wondering if I could go back to sleep myself. No. I was completely awake, eyes wide open to a long day that should have been different.

Mom sat down beside me and hugged me. "Happy birthday, sweetheart. Sixteen years old! You know, you're almost grown up." Feeling her arms around me, I knew I should be grateful for her love, that it should be enough to make me happy. But right now it just wasn't.

"How about breakfast?" she asked. "French toast?"

"That would be nice," I said, and hoped my smile looked real.

"I was thinking about what we might do today to celebrate," she said.

"It's okay. We don't have to do anything," I said. She looked disappointed. "I mean, we can make up for it next year, right?"

"What about dinner? I'll fix you something special. At least I can do that."

That night Mom laid out the white tablecloth and fixed one of the best meals she'd ever cooked. She invited Crystal and Chelsea Rose, Jan, Carlos and Alonzo. After dinner she brought out a caramel cake—my favorite—with sixteen candles.

"Rachel said I could light these long enough for you to blow them out," she said, touching a match to each wick. The flames danced. "Make a wish!"

I closed my eyes and made the wish I'd been making since we'd moved into St. Agatha's—that we could move out again soon. Then I blew.

"Woo-hoo!" Crystal shouted. "Wish come true."

"Hope it was a good one," Jan said.

"I'm gonna wish for a fire truck on my birthday," Alonzo said, reaching a finger toward the frosting. Jan slapped at his hand. "A real fire truck I can drive. You can drive it too, J-man."

Mom cut the cake and passed slices around. Then she handed me a small package.

"What's this?" I asked.

"A birthday present, of course."

"But I don't need a present. You shouldn't have spent any money on me."

"I didn't spend any money," she said. "Go ahead. Open it."

I tore off the wrapping paper and held a small gray velvet box in my palm. Inside was a gold ring with a rectangular blue stone surrounded by diamonds. "It's beautiful," I whispered.

"It was your grandmother Durbin's engagement ring," Mom said. "Your father wanted to give it to you when you turned sixteen."

I didn't remember my grandmother. She had died when I was a baby, but I had seen pictures of her, a small woman with curly blond hair and a sweet smile. Dad always said I looked like her, and maybe I did. I slipped the ring onto my finger. It fit perfectly.

"You got the skinniest fingers I've ever seen," Crystal said as I held my hand out for her to see the ring. "You could be a hand model. Hey, is it a real sapphire?"

"Sapphire and diamonds," Mom said. "You'll need to keep that in a safe place. Save it for special occasions."

"Can I wear it now?"

"Of course. Now is a special occasion. Happy birthday, sweetheart."

Before I went to sleep that night, I put the ring back in its box and hid it in a black portfolio of artwork that I kept under the bed. I lay awake for a long time thinking about the day. Being sixteen really meant something. It meant more than just being able to drive or get a job. It meant taking charge of your life. Or screwing it up. At sixteen Crystal was pregnant, Jan was dealing, Tina was

74

on the streets. I might be in a shelter, but I wasn't that messed up. I could make things happen. Good things.

I could contact my aunt Kathy and get us out.

Around four a.m. I was awakened by the fire alarm. Mom grabbed Jimmy and shouted at me to follow her out the door. Remembering that the ground was covered with snow, I slipped on my boots and grabbed the comforter and Mom's shoes. She'd forgotten to put them on. I hesitated, thinking of my ring hidden in the box under the bed, then ran out of the room after Mom and Jimmy. I'd have to let it go.

By the time I got downstairs, most of the residents were gathered in the parking lot across the street. A fire truck screamed to a stop in front of the shelter, red lights flashing. Paula was counting residents as the firefighters entered the building.

"This has happened before," Crystal told me. She had wrapped a blanket around herself and Chelsea Rose, but she was shivering.

"What, a fire?"

"You see any fire? You smell any smoke? Last summer the alarms went off about this time of night. Twice. And we all stood here for an hour while they checked things out."

"Was the alarm system broken?"

"Rachel and Paula said it had malfunctioned, but I don't believe it."

"Why not?" I asked.

"Because I've got another theory," Crystal said.

"Which is?"

"Somebody was smoking in their room or lighting a candle. Or somebody pulled the alarm."

I looked around. Mom and Jimmy were standing with Jan and Carlos. Ruthanne was wrapped in a blanket with her daughter, Marie. Alonzo stood apart from the crowd with Tina. The other women and kids were huddled together like disaster victims. Nobody was saying much.

"Why would somebody do that?" I asked.

"Who knows? For the excitement of it. Because they're pissed off." She pulled the blanket tighter around her shoulders. As we stood there in the cold, I almost wished St. Agatha's really would burn down. If we had no shelter to stay in, Mom would have to contact her sister. Wouldn't Child Protective Services or somebody force her to?

But the shelter was perfectly safe. After about half an hour a firefighter began directing everyone across the street and back into the building.

"False alarm," Paula reassured us cheerfully. "Everybody back inside where it's warm."

"False alarm," Crystal whispered. "That's all you'll hear. But I guarantee you it's more than that."

9

The next afternoon Crystal banged on the door to our room.

"You want to go somewhere?" she asked. She had Chelsea Rose bundled into her snowsuit and strapped into a baby backpack. Chelsea's blue eyes peeped out from under a pink knit cap, and her hands were covered by tiny thumbless mittens. She could hardly move.

"Where?" I asked.

"Over to Elton's."

"I didn't think you went to Elton's house," I said.

"Only when his parents are gone. Which they are. You want to come?"

"I don't know if I can."

"Of course you can." She put her hands on her hips. "Maybe you don't want to, though. Elton isn't exactly Bentley Academy material."

"I don't go to Bentley Academy," I said.

"Poor thing, and all she got for her birthday was a sapphire ring." Crystal had a way of bringing up my so-called privileged background, even though I lived in a shelter just like she did.

"Okay. I'll go, then," I said.

"Don't do me any favors. I was only thinking that you might want to get out of here for a change. See a new face."

"I said I'd go, didn't I?" I left Mom a note telling her I'd gone for a walk with Crystal, then pulled on my boots and got my coat.

"You think you could help me do some more research?" I asked as we walked along the icy sidewalk. Chelsea Rose stared at me solemnly as she bounced along in the backpack.

"You mean the Halperin Files?" Crystal said in the voice of a TV detective.

"Yeah. Could you get the address?"

"Can't you find it yourself?"

"I'm not very good with computers," I said. I'd avoided keyboarding in middle school by taking an extra art class. At Bentley we were expected to know everything already. Lots of my friends had blogs. I didn't even have an e-mail address.

"I might be able to help you," Crystal said. "It all depends."

"On what, a fee?" I asked.

"You can't get something for nothing."

"I'll babysit Chelsea Rose again," I said, and then Crystal laughed.

"Hey, I'm just playing with you." She elbowed me. "Think of it as a late birthday present."

Elton lived on the other side of Randolf High School, in what my mother would call a transitional neighborhood. Meaning the neighborhood had transitioned way down the social ladder and was tentatively creeping up again. A lot of the big Victorian houses had been cut up into apartments, but Elton's was still in one piece, a gray house with a cupola and a wraparound porch. The gingerbread trim needed paint and the steps sagged a little, but it was a cool house. Crystal pressed the doorbell, and dogs started barking inside.

"They make a lot of noise, but they're gentle as kittens," Crystal reassured me.

Elton opened the door, and two lanky bloodhounds scrambled out.

"Sarge, Dallas!" he shouted at them, and grabbed their collars. "They'll calm down once they get used to you," he said, and gave them each a little jerk. "Bad boys!"

I had never met Elton before, but I'd heard so much about him that I was surprised he didn't look at all as I'd imagined. For one thing, he looked young. Way too young to have a kid. He was skinny and kind of short, with black curls that hung over his eyes. He wore a Metallica T-shirt and jeans, and tennis shoes that looked too big for the rest of him. Once he had sent the dogs into the basement, he gave Crystal a quick kiss, then reached for Chelsea Rose.

"He's more excited about seeing her than seeing me," Crystal complained patiently as Elton pulled his daughter out of the baby backpack. "This is Lucy," she added. "In case you're interested."

"I'm interested," Elton said, and grinned at me. "Crystal's told me about you."

"Don't say that. She's stuck up enough as it is," Crystal said.

"Don't listen to her, Lucy," Elton said.

"I don't," I said. Crystal made a face at me.

"When do your parents get back?" she asked, resting the backpack against a love seat.

"Not until after dinner. We can get pizza if you want." He held Chelsea Rose in one arm and had the other wrapped around Crystal's waist. He couldn't take his eyes off her.

Elton clearly wanted some time alone with Crystal. Since St. Agatha's had a no-men-on-the-premises policy and his parents had a no-Crystal policy, they rarely found time to be by themselves in private.

"Let me see the new guitar," Crystal said, breaking the spell he seemed to be under.

"You ought to hear his band," she told me as Elton led us upstairs to a room filled with musical instruments. "He can play everything in here. He's got a gift."

"Don't believe everything you hear, Lucy," he said, and pushed his hair off his forehead. His eyes were deep blue, long and narrow, almost rectangular. For a second he looked a lot like Chelsea Rose.

Elton picked up an electric guitar and played a few chords. Then he launched into a song that I had often heard on the radio. If I hadn't known better, I'd have thought he had recorded it himself. Chelsea Rose bounced in Crystal's arms.

"Look at that," Crystal said proudly. "She's already dancing."

"Sing with me, Cryssie," Elton said, and she gave me the baby.

Elton played the first bars of "Stairway to Heaven." Anybody who can play guitar can play those first measures, but Elton made them sound new. When Crystal started singing, I was amazed. She had a wonderful voice, warm and clear. Chelsea Rose stayed perfectly still in my arms, listening to her parents make an old song sound like it had never been sung before.

"You never told me you could do that!" I said when they finished.

"You never asked," Crystal shot back, but she was smiling. "That's how me and Elton met, in chorus at Randolf. He was really shy back then, but I thought he was just the cutest thing." Elton's pale cheeks turned bright pink.

"When was that?" I asked.

"Sophomore year. We were your age." She made it sound like she was way older than me, and in some ways I guess she was. "Elton was afraid to ask me out. I had to put the moves on him."

"How long did you go out before, well, you know?"

"About a year and a half," Elton said, ignoring my awkwardness. "Chelsea was born in July."

"His parents deal with the situation mainly by pretending it never happened," Crystal said. "And they think I'm a slut."

"As soon as I graduate, I'll move out," Elton said.

"We're getting married this summer," Crystal added. "You want to come to the wedding?"

"Sure," I said, surprised by the casual invitation. Chelsea Rose started fussing, so I gave her to Crystal.

"Time for dinner, sweet pea?" she asked the baby, and sat down on the couch. "I know I'm trying to wean her, but it's so easy this way." She reached under her shirt and unhooked her bra. "This child is going to be as big as Carlos, the way she eats." I looked away as she got Chelsea Rose situated under her shirt.

"What kind of pizza do you want?" Elton asked.

"I've got to go," I said, feeling out of place. "But thanks."

"You sure?" Crystal said. "You don't want to hang out?"

"I need to get back and take care of Jimmy while Mom studies."

"You ought to come out with Crystal and hear the band sometime," Elton said as I put my coat on. "We play at the Yellow Door most Saturdays."

"Thanks," I said, wondering what Mom would say to that. "Maybe I will."

"Did you and Crystal have a nice walk?" Mom asked as I came in. "Where did you go?"

"Just around," I said. I hadn't even closed the door and she was already full of questions. "I met Crystal's boyfriend."

Mom's mouth tightened a little. "And is he nice?"

"Yeah. We went over to his house. I was invited to stay for dinner, but I thought I'd better come back."

"I thought his parents didn't like Crystal," Mom said.

"They weren't there." As soon as I said it, I knew I shouldn't have.

"I'm not sure I like the idea of you being in some boy's house without his parents at home."

"Mom, he and Crystal are parents themselves! They're practically married," I said. "You'd like him, Mom. You'd be proud of Crystal for making such a good choice."

Mom didn't say anything.

"Where's Jimmy?" I asked.

"I let him go sledding with Jan and the boys. They ought to be home soon."

"He's doing pretty well here, don't you think?" I said.

"At least one of us seems to have adjusted," she said, smiling faintly. "And that's better than nothing."

10

n the six months I'd been at Randolf High, I'd never noticed Elton, but now I ran into him all the time. Elton looked like every other skinny, long-haired heavy-metal fan. But once he turned those strange blue eyes on you, you never forgot him. I was beginning to see why Crystal had put the moves on him, as she said.

"You know him?" Aspen asked a few days after I'd been to Elton's house. We were sitting on the front steps of Randolf, and Elton had stopped to say hi before he went inside. People always stopped to talk to Aspen; it was rare for someone to speak to me.

"He's a friend of a friend," I said. "You know him too?"

"Everybody knows Elton. Because of his band," Aspen said. "Bogus Orange. Have you ever heard them?"

I shook my head.

"We ought to go sometime. He's incredible on the

guitar. Plus we used to skateboard and stuff when we were kids. Now he's got a kid himself."

"Yeah, that's how I know him."

"Through the kid?"

"The mom. She's a friend of mine."

"Really? How do you know her?"

"I live with her," I said.

We were sharing a Thermos of hot chocolate before school started. Aspen's mother sent him to school every day with enough to feed an army.

"Hey, I think I found you a job," he said suddenly.

"Really?" I had told Aspen about my birthday resolution to stop wishing and start doing something about my life. He'd encouraged me, but I didn't know he'd had his eyes open for an opportunity.

"Yeah, Ann's friend Linda owns an art supply store. She needs somebody to come in at three every afternoon so she can get her kids to piano lessons and stuff." Aspen always referred to his mother by her first name, Ann. She was a psychologist, and I guess she believed in total equality for kids, or something progressive like that. "You interested?"

"Where's the store?"

"It's only a few blocks from here. If you want to, we can go by there tomorrow afternoon."

I was about to say okay, when Mariah, one of the art room regulars, came up and grabbed his coat sleeve. "Party at Ryan's on Saturday night. You coming?"

"I don't know," Aspen said, and glanced at me. I stared at the cars across the street.

"You should come. A couple of guys from Canada may show up." She laughed like they had some inside joke.

"I'll see what I can do," Aspen said.

"I'd go if I were you." She tugged on his sleeve again, then sauntered off to join a group of girls.

"You want to go?" he asked me.

"Not really," I said quickly. Mariah could have invited me herself. Instead I felt like some kind of pet Aspen could bring if he wanted to. "What's that about Canada, anyway?"

Aspen laughed. "Ryan runs a little import business."

"What does he import?"

"What do you think?" Aspen grinned.

I shrugged. Though Aspen seemed to think I should know, I was clueless.

"Weed. He gets it from British Columbia and makes a nice profit selling it here."

"Have you ever, like, bought any?" I asked, trying not to seem shocked. Ryan was in my math class, and he seemed like a pretty smart guy.

"I don't do it that much anymore. I did freshman year. Ann calls it my aimless year, but not so much now." He took my hand. "Does that bother you?"

"I—No. I mean, it's your life." The conversation was getting awkward, and I was glad when the bell rang. I don't know why it surprised me that Aspen smoked weed. With his hair and piercings he looked like a stoner, but he never seemed messed up. But then neither did Ryan. Whether Aspen did drugs or not wasn't my concern. It wasn't like we were going out. We just ate lunch together. I hardly knew him. Apparently. He could do whatever he wanted.

And if that included helping me find a job, that was fine with me.

The next afternoon Aspen took me to Linda's Art Supply. One glance at the tubes of paint lined up in rainbow order, the stacks of paper and gum erasers, and I knew it was the job for me.

"Aspen tells me you take a painting class with him at Randolf," Linda said after she had finished showing me around. "Who do you have right now?"

"Ms. Ashland," I said. "I like her. She's real no-nonsense."

"Yeah, and Lucy's teacher's pet," Aspen teased.

"That's not true," I said.

"It is. She's really good," Aspen said. "Show her your sketchbook."

At Linda's encouragement I pulled my sketchbook out of my backpack. Linda turned the pages slowly. "You've got talent," she said. "These faces, are they portraits or just made up?"

"Some are people I know. Some are just made up."

"What about this one?" she asked, looking at the picture of my father.

"Someone I know," I said.

Linda told me to come in the next Monday. She would pay me minimum wage and give me a twenty percent discount on all merchandise. I didn't bother to tell her I couldn't afford to buy anything, even at twenty percent off. My plan was to save every penny I earned until we were out of St. Agatha's. I figured I could make thirty to forty dollars a week. It wasn't much. I used to spend that much on makeup and CDs and other piddly stuff in a week, easy. But it was better than nothing. It was a start.

"I don't know about you having a job," Mom said when I told her I'd been hired.

"Why not? We need the money."

"But with work and school, when will you have time for other things?"

"What other things?" I said bluntly. Sometimes Mom seemed to forget we weren't in Andover Hills anymore.

"Okay, but if your grades start to fall—"

"They won't. I've got better grades than I had last year," I reminded her.

She sighed. "Your father wouldn't have liked you working."

"He should have thought of that before he blew our money."

"Lucy!"

"Well, it's true, isn't it?" I tried to control my voice. "Isn't it?"

"Your father—" she began, then stopped.

"My father what?" I asked.

She didn't answer.

By the middle of March I'd gotten used to the store and Linda, who was a little compulsive and overly organized, but nice. Since she kept things so neat, my job was easy. Usually there wasn't much traffic, maybe three or four customers in an afternoon. After my first week Linda trusted me to lock up at five every day. Aspen came by most afternoons after Linda left to pick up her kids. He'd bring me a chai tea or a latte, hang around and talk. Whether or not he went to the "import" party at Ryan's never came up. I tried not to think about what he was doing on the weekends, but it wasn't easy. Then something happened that made it even harder.

One afternoon when I went into the stockroom for some erasers, he followed me. He closed the door behind him.

"What are you doing?" I asked, and laughed as he took my hands.

"Something I've been wanting to do for a while," he said, and then he kissed me. I'd been kissed before, but not like this. Kissing Aspen felt like something I should have been doing for a long time. Something I didn't want to stop doing.

After that first day, that first kiss, I'd restock the shelves and dust as fast as I could, and then he'd come in the front door, ringing the little bells that hung on the handle, and we'd find ourselves in the stockroom. If a customer came in, I'd hear the bells and leave Aspen in the dark. When the customer left, I'd slip back into the room, into Aspen and his warm breath against my neck, and the way he smelled like woodsmoke and cloves.

Some days we'd linger after the doors were locked, and then he'd drive me to the corner a couple of blocks from the shelter and let me out to walk the rest of the way home. Getting out of the car early was my choice. He would have taken me to the doorstep if I'd let him. But for some reason it was important to keep him separate from St. Agatha's. He was connected to a different part of my life, a private part that I didn't want to share, especially not with my mom.

"You're home late," Mom said one day. She was sitting at the desk with her math book open in front of her. Jimmy lay on the floor cutting people out of a magazine.

"Linda wanted me to inventory some stock," I lied, not looking at her.

"You should call and let me pick you up. It's too dark to be walking alone."

"Okay," I said, not wanting to prolong the conversation. "Next time I'll call."

Mom wouldn't have cared that I was interested in someone. I'd gone out with the captain of Bentley's JV basketball team for a couple of months. A junior had taken me to the Christmas party at the country club freshman year. Even though I'd liked these guys okay, I'd never really cared about them. I cared about Aspen a lot. And it scared me. I knew what Mom would say if she met him. She'd criticize his clothes and his hair. She'd be appalled at the silver hoop in his eyebrow. She'd assume he used drugs and was going nowhere. She might tell me I couldn't see him anymore. At best she'd worry, and she didn't need to worry any more than she already was. She needed to concentrate on school and getting us out of St. Agatha's.

"How was class today?" I asked her, and took the scissors and the magazine from Jimmy. I cut out a man pushing a lawn mower and gave it to him.

"All right, I guess. I just wish I liked the material

better." She stared at her textbook. "Do you think I'll have to use this stuff once I get a job?"

I shrugged. "Depends on the job." I tried to picture my mother in a cubicle, her hands on a keyboard, but it was too depressing.

"What's for dinner?" I asked, hoping a change of subject would put her in a better mood.

"Is it time for dinner already?" She looked at her watch and sighed. "I don't know. Something fast and easy."

"Chicken noodle soup!" Jimmy shouted.

"Soup's fine with me," I said. What I really wanted was fettuccine with a nice Alfredo sauce and homemade bread. But Mom hadn't made a real dinner since my birthday. We were eating like everyone else in the shelter. Only Jimmy seemed to be thriving on oatmeal, canned soup, and mac and cheese.

Despite my worries about Mom finding out about Aspen, I agreed to meet him at the cineplex one Saturday afternoon for a movie. I told Mom I wanted to treat Jimmy to a matinee, which was true. I'd saved up more than I had expected. So when Aspen asked if I wanted to go to a party that weekend, I suggested a movie instead.

"During the day?" he asked. "Afraid I'll turn into a vampire at night?"

"I promised Jimmy I'd take him," I said.

"Okay, so it's a matinee," he said. "I'll pick you up."

"We'll meet you there," I said quickly.

"Whatever." He frowned, but he didn't argue.

• • •

"You want popcorn, Jimbo?" Aspen asked as he handed me the tickets.

"Yeah, and a drink." Jimmy looked up at me. "Is it okay to have a Sprite, Lucy?"

I was about to say no, but Aspen said sure, Jimmy could have anything he wanted.

At first Jimmy had stared at Aspen, but after Aspen started talking to him, he warmed up. I had told Jimmy that Aspen was a friend from school, but that we wouldn't talk about him to Mom. I reminded him how busy Mom was with her classes, that she didn't have time right now to meet our new friends.

Jimmy gently touched Aspen's hair. "How did you get it to grow like caterpillars on your head?"

"Elves," Aspen said, and winked. "They got in my bed one night and I woke up like this." Jimmy laughed and rubbed his own unruly red hair as Aspen headed for the long line at the concession stand.

Jimmy and I found a bench in the lobby. A group of people from Randolf walked by and waved. I waved back and watched them get in line behind Aspen, who turned to talk to them. I was wondering what they were laughing at, when I heard my name.

"Lucy?" Amanda, Kari and another girl from Bentley, Sylvia Tate, stood in front of me. Amanda and Kari used to call Sylvia a satellite, someone who orbited around the popular crowd but wasn't really part of it. I'd secretly liked Sylvia, but I was surprised to see her hanging out with my old friends.

"Wow, I wasn't sure that was you. I thought I recognized your brother," Amanda said.

"Oh, hi." I forced myself to smile. They weren't sure it was me? Did I really look that different?

"You're letting your hair grow out," Kari said, and wrinkled her nose.

"It looks good," Sylvia added.

"Thanks," I said, trying to tuck the loose ends behind my ears. Amanda and Kari were scrutinizing my clothes. The eighties jacket I'd thought was kind of cool when I found it in the clothing room suddenly felt shabby, and I was very aware how out-dated my jeans were.

"So, how do you like Randolf?" Sylvia asked, filling the silence that was threatening to engulf us.

"Isn't it awfully inner city?" Amanda asked, before I could answer. She made little quotation marks in the air when she said *inner city*.

"It's downtown, if that's what you mean," I said.

"No, I mean like gangs and stuff. You know, ethnic problems," Amanda said.

"I've heard the art teachers are good," Sylvia offered, but Kari and Amanda weren't interested in Randolf's positive aspects.

"I heard they have metal detectors at the doors," Kari added. "I heard a kid pulled a gun on a teacher there last year."

"I don't know about that," I said. "I wasn't there last year."

"Aren't there a lot of drugs?" Amanda asked.

"No more than at Bentley," I said sharply.

"Really?" She smiled the fake smile I was so familiar with. The one reserved for satellites and other people who didn't matter.

93

"Yeah, really. I like Randolf," I said. "I'm happy there."

"Really?" Amanda said again. Just then Aspen walked up with a tub of popcorn and two sodas, and I introduced him. The girls eyed his dreadlocks and the silver hoop, but as soon as he smiled, I could see interest in their faces. His beautiful eyes, his slow lazy grin—even they were charmed. Kari lowered her eyelids shyly, then looked up quickly, directly into his face. It was her flirty look, but it actually made her look like one of her contacts had slipped. Amanda held out her hand, and Aspen gave me the popcorn tub so he could shake hands with her. That was so Amanda. Having to touch every guy she met. Like marking territory.

"It was so good to see you, Lucy," she said, suddenly sweet and gracious. "Call me."

"We'll go shopping," Kari added, and flashed her eyes at Aspen again before she and Amanda walked off. Sylvia lingered for a moment.

"I'm glad I ran into you," she said. "If you ever want to hang out, or just talk . . ." She gave my arm a squeeze and hurried after the other two.

Of the three of them she was the only one who meant what she said. I took a deep breath and clenched my hands together to keep them from shaking.

"You okay?" Aspen asked.

"Yeah. It's just weird to see them."

"They're people you knew at Bentley, aren't they?"

"They used to be my best friends," I said, and my eyes burned for a second.

"Forget about them." Aspen took my hand. "You've got a new best friend now."

II

"I've got something for you," Crystal said one morning before school. She handed me a printout from the *Seattle Times* online. The headline read, HOME TOUR SHOWCASES WATERFRONT ARCHITECTURE. She pointed to the third paragraph. *Included in the tour will be the award-winning home of Wilson and Kathy Halperin.*

"Okay, so what should I do with this?" I asked.

"Don't you want to see what might happen if you meet her?"

"During a home tour? Kind of public, don't you think? And what about a ticket? Those things usually cost something." Our house had been on a holiday tour two years ago. Ironically, the event had been a benefit for a place very much like the one we were living in now.

"It tells you where to call to reserve one." She pointed to the bottom of the article.

"Twenty-five dollars? That's a lot of money," I said, not sure I wanted to do something like this. "And how am I supposed to get to Seattle?"

"Elton has a car. He'll drive us."

"Us?"

"You, me and Chelsea. I need a change of scenery," she said. "Oh, come on, Lucy. It'll be an adventure!"

"What are you doing Saturday?" I asked Aspen the next afternoon. He'd brought me a cup of chai tea at work and was sitting on the checkout counter while I opened rolls of coins for the cash register.

"The usual. Sleeping till noon, then eating a bowl of Lucky Charms. After that I don't know," he said.

"I'm serious."

"Why? Are you asking me on a date?"

"I was thinking about a road trip to Seattle," I said. "You got other plans?"

Aspen shrugged. "What's in Seattle?" he asked. I showed him the article from the *Times* and told him about my aunt and the home tour.

"Crystal said Elton could drive us," I said. "You want to come?"

"I guess. Seems kind of risky, though, a bunch of scruffy-looking strangers just showing up like that."

"We're not all going to show up at her house, just me." Crystal and I had it all figured out. If we left at nine, we'd get there in plenty of time for me to catch the end of the home tour. Elton would drop me off and they'd find something to do for an hour or so. I'd just kind of hang around until the crowd cleared out and I could talk to Kathy alone.

Aspen hopped off the counter. "Okay, I'll go. Ann will be glad to see me out of bed before one o'clock."

I could only hope Kathy would be glad to see me.

I told Mom that Linda needed me at the store on Saturday. There was a chance she'd call me there, but I figured it was a risk worth taking. Mom had never called the store before, why would she start now? The more I thought about the trip, the more excited I got. Things could really change for us. I didn't expect Kathy to actually give us money, but a loan was possible, wasn't it? And once Mom got the loan, she couldn't be mad at me.

Saturday I dressed in black pants and the red sweater the Mercedes lady with the Nordstrom bags had dropped off. While Mom was taking a shower, I pulled my portfolio out from under my bed and took the sapphire ring from its hiding place. I slipped it into my coat pocket along with pearl earrings and a gold bracelet; I had asked Crystal to bring my Kate Spade handbag. Mom always noticed what I had on, down to the smallest detail, and I didn't want her to get suspicious.

"I'll be back by dinner," I told her.

"You sure you don't want a ride?" she asked.

"I need the exercise," I said. "See you about six."

Elton's old black Subaru was waiting around the corner. He'd picked up Crystal and Chelsea Rose a few minutes earlier. We drove east toward Maple Street and Aspen's house. When we got there, I climbed the stone steps and rang the bell. Aspen's mom opened the door.

"You must be Lucy," she said, and invited me in. "Aspen's running a little late."

"That's okay." I sat on the edge of the couch. Aspen's house looked like him, kind of odd and rambling, with dark wood trim and lots of pictures on the walls. "You have some nice paintings," I said nervously.

"Thanks. I'm a little impulsive when it comes to buying art. I always wanted to paint, but my talents seem to lie elsewhere."

"You're a therapist, right?" I asked.

"Yes. I work with children," Ann said, and I wondered if Aspen had told her about me, the homeless girl. How would she analyze me? A white dog trotted into the room, his toenails clicking on the hardwood floor. He sniffed my boots and looked up expectantly.

"Bobby's spoiled, you'll have to excuse his manners." Ann laughed. "I can't do a thing with him. Kind of like my son." She went to the bottom of the stairs and yelled for Aspen to hurry up.

"He's always late." She shrugged apologetically, then said, "I may be confusing you with someone else, but are you the one who works for Linda Pullman?"

I said I was, and wondered who she might be confusing me with. Mariah? One of the other girls Aspen was so friendly with? And then Aspen bounded down the stairs and we were on our way.

. . .

Until you get to the mountains, the scenery from Cottonwood Falls to Seattle is pretty dull, especially when it's covered with old snow. Crystal sat in the front with Elton. Chelsea Rose's car seat was buckled in the back with me and Aspen. Once we got out of town, Chelsea Rose fell asleep. I rested my head on Aspen's shoulder. He put his arm around me.

"Nervous?" he asked.

"Yeah. I have no idea what I'll say to her."

"You'll do fine. She'll meet you and she'll have to do the right thing."

"I wish I knew what happened between her and Mom," I said.

"Whatever it was happened a long time ago. Which is good. People get over things. Maybe she'll be glad to see you."

"Maybe." I took the sapphire ring out of my pocket and slipped it on my left hand.

"Pretty," Aspen said, holding my hand close to examine the ring.

"It was my grandmother's. Maybe it will bring me good luck."

We crossed the Cascades before noon. There was light snow falling on the pass, which slowed us down some. As we descended on the west side of the mountains, rain took the place of snow, and then the sun broke through the clouds and I had a good feeling about what the afternoon would bring.

. . .

All the houses on the tour were in the same general location on the banks of Lake Washington. Wide green lawns and curved driveways led to massive front doors. Blue water sparkled behind them. At a brown and cream Tudor with ivy climbing up the wall, I picked up my reserved ticket and a tour brochure; then Elton drove along the lakeshore to Kathy Halperin's house.

"Wow, that's some house," Crystal said as Elton stopped in front of a large gray building.

"It's huge," I said. The brochure described it as *minimalist contemporary*. It looked like a futuristic fortress.

"Don't let it freak you out, Lucy," she said. "It's just a house."

"Good luck," Aspen said, and squeezed my hand as I got out of the car.

I took a deep breath as the Subaru pulled away from the curb. The tour wasn't over for another hour, which should give me enough time to wander around some and then introduce myself as the crowd was leaving. How much I told Kathy about our situation would depend on how much she seemed willing to hear. But given the size of her house, given the fact that she and her husband donated so much money to the arts, I felt certain she'd be willing to help. If all went well, we could be out of St. Agatha's by the summer.

As I followed the line of home-tourists up the flagstone path through the terraced yard, my heart was pounding. Wearing the black leather jacket Dad had given me last year for my birthday, I hoped I looked sophisticated and mature, not like a nervous teenager. A guest book lay on a table in the foyer. Should I sign it?

What if she saw my name? Did she even know my name? All of a sudden I was in a panic. Would she believe me when I told her who I was?

Kathy Halperin stood in the foyer greeting her guests. I recognized her right away from the photos. She smiled at me and told me she was delighted I had come. She smiled at the couple behind me and told them the same thing. She was wearing a gray cashmere dress, pearls, and beautiful leather shoes. Her hair was expertly tinted, her frosty nails manicured. When she turned her face in profile, she looked so much like Mom that a wave of anxiety swept through me. But I smiled and nodded and followed the trail of visitors through the first floor and up the stairs. I lingered at the end of the line, then ducked into one of the bedrooms and pretended to look at some Japanese paintings. Only ten more minutes until the tour was officially over. In ten minutes I'd go downstairs and talk to her.

Then suddenly she was standing at the doorway.

"Aren't they lovely?" She nodded at the paintings above the bed. "Wilson got them in Kyoto."

"They're beautiful," I said. "The brushwork is so delicate."

She stood beside me for a moment admiring her paintings; then she turned and smiled at me.

"Have I met you before?"

"Um, I don't think so. I'm just visiting Seattle." This is my opportunity, I thought frantically. How can I make the best impression?

"You look so familiar," she said. "I must be mistaking you for someone else."

"I'm Lucy Durbin," I said, and turned directly toward her, not knowing any other way to introduce myself. "Cindy is my mother."

Kathy Halperin sat down slowly in a small chair. Her face blanched under the careful makeup. For a moment she closed her eyes.

"You're Cindy's daughter," she murmured. "That's why you look so familiar." She was about to say something more, but her husband came into the room with two older women.

"Honey, these ladies especially wanted to see the Kyoto paintings. Want to fill them in?" He looked at her carefully. "Are you feeling all right?"

"I'm fine. I was just talking to one of our guests." She smiled at me. "It's Lucy, right?"

I nodded, admiring the way she instantly regained her composure, like a figure skater regaining her balance after a difficult maneuver. I waited as she told the women about the artist, and her husband led them back downstairs.

"How is Cindy?" Kathy asked. There was an empty chair next to hers, but she didn't ask me to sit down. I stood awkwardly in front of her.

"Fine," I said, then added, "She's taking Dad's death pretty well."

"I was sorry to hear about that," she said, but she sounded more irritated than sad.

"It was totally unexpected." How much should I tell her? "In fact," I continued, "it was so unexpected that we weren't really very prepared."

"No one is ever prepared for that kind of loss," she said, and I could tell she wasn't getting it.

"We—We had to move from our house," I faltered. "It's been kind of difficult. Financially, I mean."

Kathy raised her eyebrows and pressed her lips together.

"But we're doing okay," I added quickly. Pleading financial difficulties wasn't the strategy to use. I pushed my hair back with my left hand so she could see the sapphire ring. She stared at the ring for a long minute, then looked at me with an expression I couldn't read.

"Well, it was nice of you to stop by." She stood up abruptly and began herding me toward the door. "But it's time to end the tour now."

My legs felt weak as I went downstairs to the foyer. Without touching me, Kathy Halperin was pushing me out of her house.

"Could I come back some other time?" I asked, feeling my chance slip away.

"I don't think that would be a good idea."

"I'm sorry to just show up this way," I said, trying to keep the desperation out of my voice. "I realize it was kind of a surprise."

My aunt wasn't smiling anymore. She opened the front door and a cold wind blew in. "Did your mother send you here?" she asked.

"No. She doesn't even know I came!"

She paused for a moment, then said, "Well, you might want to keep it that way."

"I'm sorry, I thought maybe you'd want to know—"

"Your mother and I . . . ," she began, and then her voice changed. "This really isn't a good time. Now, if you'll excuse me."

I nodded, but she didn't see me. She had already closed the door.

12

I was so shocked at the way my aunt treated me that I went down the wrong path through the terraced lawn. Instead of leaving her property, I ended up in the back-yard. Terrified that she would spot me and think I was lurking around, I ducked into some bushes until I could get my bearings. It had started to rain, and I wandered through the wet dark leaves until I found myself in the front yard again. When Elton's old black Subaru pulled up to the curb, I ran toward it.

"How'd it go?" Crystal asked excitedly as I got into the car. Then she saw my face. "God, what happened?"

All I could do was burst into tears. Aspen put his arms around me and stroked my damp hair. "You want Elton to stop the car for a minute? You need to walk around?"

I shook my head. "Just drive."

I stared through the rain-streaked window at the big

houses, the perfect lawns. All I wanted to do was get as far away from Kathy Halperin and her big cold house as I could. As we drove out of Seattle, no one said much. Chelsea Rose sucked contentedly on a pacifier. Crystal kept changing the CD impatiently. I felt guilty for acting like a baby. They had made this trip for me. I owed them some kind of explanation, but I couldn't talk about it.

As we climbed into the Cascade Mountains, the rain turned to snow. By the time we reached North Bend, it was coming down hard. Elton turned off the CD player.

"Find the weather station, Cryssie," he said. "It's on AM, around fifteen hundred." Crystal found the station and we listened to a recorded voice tell us that snow and sleet had been falling on Snoqualmie Pass for two hours. The road was iced over at the summit and chains were strongly advised.

"I don't have chains," Elton muttered. Traffic had slowed to a crawl. As we climbed higher, we saw a couple of cars spinning their wheels on the median. A tow truck passed us, yellow lights flashing.

"Maybe we should turn around," Crystal said.

"We can't. There's no off-ramp. We're in the goddamn mountains," Elton said through clenched teeth.

"Just go for it," Aspen said. "You've got four-wheel drive."

Elton caught my eye in the rearview mirror. I tried to smile.

"Hey, don't worry, Lucy," he said. "I'll get us over the pass."

And he did. It took us an hour, but we made it over the Cascades.

Still, we hadn't made it home yet. It was almost six, and Mom would be expecting me. By now it was dark, and the snow hadn't let up. Elton hunched over the steering wheel, trying to see through the half circles cleared by his windshield wipers. We passed more cars stalled on the shoulder of the highway, heard sirens and saw flashing lights. Chelsea Rose slept through it all.

In Ellensburg we pulled in at a Zip Mart. Crystal took Chelsea Rose into the ladies' room to change her diaper while Elton pumped gas.

"You better call your mom," Aspen said, and handed me his cell. "There's no way we'll be home before nine."

I dialed the number of St. Agatha's. "Room number twelve," I said to Rachel, hoping she wouldn't recognize my voice.

"Hey, Lucy," Rachel said. "Your mom's been looking for you. Everything okay?" She sounded concerned.

"Everything's fine," I lied. "Could you get her for me?"

"Hey, it's me," I said when Mom answered.

"Where in the world are you?" she said. "I thought you'd be home by now."

"I'm going to be late."

"I called the store and you weren't there. Where are you?"

"I'm in Ellensburg."

"Ellensburg! What are you doing there?"

"We're coming home as fast as we can. We ran into some bad weather." The phone was starting to break up. I got out of the car, hoping for a better connection. "Can you hear me?"

"Who are you with?"

"Elton and Crystal. We had to come here—" I tried to think of a reason I might be in Ellensburg. But she interrupted me.

"I've been so worried! What is going on?"

"I'm sorry. I'll explain when I get home."

She said something else, but I couldn't hear her.

"Mom?" I shouted into the phone. "Can you hear me? I'm really sorry!" The connection went dead. Snow was driving against my face and I was freezing. My expensive leather coat and boots might look good, but they weren't much help against a blizzard.

"Bad news," Elton said when he came out of the store. "They've had to close the bridge over the Columbia. A semi flipped in Vantage and it's blocking the highway. We could try another route, but I think we're better off sticking to the interstate."

"Yeah, the other roads will definitely be worse," Aspen said.

Crystal gave me a sympathetic look and shrugged. "I guess we're here for a while."

"Well, it looks pretty bad for now," Elton said. "But it's not forever."

"God, Elton! Sometimes you are so lame." Crystal smacked his arm.

"You guys want to get something to eat?" Aspen said. "I'm starving."

We bought shrink-wrapped sandwiches and hot chocolate from a machine and sat down at one of the vinyl booths in the back of the Zip Mart.

"If you don't want to talk about it, that's okay," Crystal began. "But what the hell happened back there?"

I took a deep breath. "She threw me out."

"Your aunt threw you out?" Aspen said. "That is really harsh."

"I don't know what I was thinking. She doesn't even know me. She never wanted to know me. Why should she want to help me?"

"What did she say?" Crystal asked, and I told them how in less than fifteen minutes I'd met my aunt and been invited off her property.

"No shit," Crystal said. "Did she threaten you with a restraining order or anything?"

I blinked, then shook my head.

"Man, that definitely sucks. I'm really sorry for even suggesting this plan," Crystal said.

"It's not your fault. I'm the one who got swept up in some stupid family fantasy. I should have listened to my mom. She said to leave her sister alone."

"Well, you gave it a try," Elton said. "Now you know."

"Yeah, there's something in knowing the truth," Aspen added.

Or part of the truth, I thought. I knew Kathy didn't want to help us, but I didn't know why.

We sat at the booth long after our sandwiches were gone. A few other snow refugees were hanging out eating and playing the one video game next to the men's room. Elton struck up a conversation with the guy behind the counter and was getting weather and traffic updates as they came over the store's scanner. It was clear the bridge would be closed until the next morning.

"I am not spending the night in a Zip Mart," Crystal said.

"Maybe we could try that place over there." Aspen pointed to a Motel 6 across the road.

"At least we could get some sleep," Elton said. "I'm pretty wiped out. How much money do we have?" We emptied our pockets and counted our change. It looked like we had enough for one room. While Crystal bought diapers, I called St. Agatha's again. For once I was glad there were no private lines in the rooms. I left a message with Paula, who had replaced Rachel by this time, saying we were snowbound and I'd be home as soon as I could. Paula wanted to call Mom to the phone, but I said no. What would be the point?

"Take your pick, Lucy," Crystal said, gesturing to the two double beds in the motel room. "I'm afraid with Chelsea Rose here we won't be getting a lot of sleep."

Chelsea Rose had opened her eyes as soon as we got into the room and, as Crystal said, she was ready to party. Aspen sat in front of the TV for a few minutes flipping through the channels. Not that any of us wanted to watch anything. It was just something to do until we got used to the idea of spending the night in the same room. I took off my coat and boots and lay down on top of the covers.

"You might as well get in all the way," Aspen said, tugging on the bedspread. "We can put a pillow between us if you want."

"It's okay," I said. "I just want it to be morning so we can get home."

He turned off the TV and lay down next to me. He'd taken off his shoes, but otherwise he was fully dressed. "I could sleep on the floor," he offered.

"I'll trust you to stay on your side of the bed," I said, and smiled. He took my hand and kissed it as Elton turned off the light.

Elton and Crystal, with Chelsea Rose, climbed into the other bed. For a few minutes we all lay silently in the dark. Then Crystal started to giggle.

"I've been waiting for two years to get Elton in bed with me for the night," she said. "And now that I've finally managed it, I've got an audience!"

Even though I was dead tired, I hardly slept. I lay there looking at Aspen in the dull glow of the streetlights, studying the little bump in his nose, the curve of his lower lip, trying to memorize the way his eyelashes curled. When the alarm clock's green numbers read six, I went into the bathroom and washed my face. I wished for a toothbrush, but that was another thing I'd just have to do without.

According to the morning news, the bridge at Vantage had been reopened. We grabbed donuts and bad coffee at the Zip Mart and started for home.

When we arrived at St. Agatha's, Aspen kissed me. "Call me later," he said.

"If I can," I answered, hoping Mom wasn't looking out the window.

Crystal pressed the button on the call box, and Rachel met us at the door.

"We were so worried," she said. "But nobody can control the weather. Glad you're safe."

"Thanks. Where's Mom?"

"She's upstairs," Rachel said.

"Good luck," Crystal whispered, and squeezed my arm.

13

"Go play with Carlos," Mom told Jimmy as soon as I came in. Jimmy stared out from under his blanket house. Even he seemed to know what kind of trouble I was in.

"What were you thinking?" Mom asked when the door closed behind him. She was trying not to raise her voice. "How could you possibly leave town without asking my permission?"

"I don't know," I said. "I didn't think you'd find out. I thought we could make it to Seattle and back before six o'clock."

"Seattle? You said Ellensburg. You were in Seattle?"

I took a deep breath. "Earlier, yes. But when I called you, I was in Ellensburg." Lying was going to be too hard. I was way too tired to try to make up something believable.

"What were you doing in Seattle?" Mom asked.

"I went to see Kathy," I said.

"You what?" Mom was shouting now.

"It was a huge mistake. I'm sorry."

"I told you not to contact her," Mom said. "You have no idea what kind of person you're dealing with."

I have some idea, I thought.

"How did you even find her?" Mom asked.

"Internet." I felt like a fine wire, buzzing, about to snap in two.

"Tell me," Mom said, her voice quiet and cold now. "Just tell me what you did."

I told her about the house tour, about introducing myself. "And then she threw me out," I finished. "Why does she hate us so much?"

"I don't want to talk about it," Mom said.

"Why not?" I asked. "I just told you everything! Why can't you tell me this one thing?"

"You told me everything? Did you tell me you were leaving town? Where you were going? What else didn't you tell me, Lucy?" An image of Aspen sleeping beside me flashed through my mind. I wished I could be with him, away from the shelter, away from my mother. I lay facedown on my bed and waited for her to leave the room.

For a couple of hours I slept. When I woke up, it was like waking into a bad dream. I wished I could go back to sleep, wished I could sleep through the next month or year or the rest of my life. I dragged myself to the bathroom and stood under the shower, hoping the hot water would drain the tiredness out of my arms and legs, but it just made me feel heavy, like a soaked towel. We were stuck at St. Agatha's, trapped in a long dark tunnel that, I finally understood, was bricked up at the end.

After telling me once to get up and get ready for school the next morning, Mom ignored me. When I finally woke up, Mom and Jimmy were gone.

"You've got to help me," I said when I found Crystal sitting at one of the tables in the library. I had to find out what had gone on between my mom and her sister. Maybe I couldn't change anything, but I needed to understand.

She gave me a fierce look and pointed at her kitchen timer. Seventeen minutes left before she'd let me talk to her. Ripping a piece of notebook paper out of her binder, I started drawing. When the egg timer went off, I had a picture of Kathy Halperin in pearls and pointy shoes blocking a doorway.

"That's her?" Crystal asked as she closed her math book.

"That's her."

"Looking like the bitch she is," Crystal said, and drew little devil horns on her forehead. I balled up the paper and threw it in the wastebasket.

"You've got to help me find out what happened between her and my mom," I said.

"Why don't you just ask your mom?"

"I did ask her. She won't tell me," I said. "But you can find out for me, Crystal. You can find out anything."

"I doubt we're going to find anything on the Web about that."

"Couldn't we just try?"

She sighed. "Let me go check on Chelsea Rose. You

get online. The *Seattle Times* seems like a logical place to start."

I turned on a computer and found the newspaper's Web page.

"When do you think they had their fight?" Crystal asked when she came back and settled down next to me in front of the computer. Chelsea Rose fidgeted on her lap.

"Maybe before I was born."

Crystal clicked on the free archives icon. "It only goes back eighteen years, but we can try."

She typed in Kathy's name and waited. Chelsea Rose was fretting on her lap, then crying, then suddenly screaming. It was impossible for Crystal to do anything.

"She's hungry again," Crystal said. "I've got to get her a bottle."

"Just feed her here."

"I'm trying to wean her."

"You've been trying to do that ever since I've known you," I said.

"Hey, it's not all that easy," she said. "You ought to try having a baby hanging on your boobs half the day! It's like having an extra body part! You ought to try making her shut up when all she wants is you!"

"Sorry. I didn't mean—" I stopped, suddenly afraid I'd say the wrong thing.

"Mean what?" Crystal said.

"I don't know. I thought I'd get everything fixed by going to Seattle, and it just made things worse." I put my head in my hands. "I hate it here."

"You think I like it?" Crystal said. "Every morning I wake up and I think, Can I stand another day without

Elton? Every night I go to bed wanting him so bad it hurts. We ought to be living in a little house with a picket fence and a goddamn cat! But I'm stuck here and he's stuck with his asshole parents." Chelsea Rose screamed even louder. "I've got to go," Crystal said.

"Wait! What do I do?"

"Follow the prompts!" she shouted over Chelsea Rose's screams. "You're not helpless, you know."

I took a deep breath and typed *Katherine Halperin*. I could do this. I could find out. A handful of matches appeared on the screen—legal stuff, charities. Nothing that would tell me why she and Mom weren't speaking. *What's the point, anyway?* I thought. Knowing why they weren't speaking wasn't going to change anything. It was a stupid idea.

And then I realized what I was doing wrong. I typed in *Katherine Sinclair* and waited.

SINCLAIR-DURBIN ENGAGED TO WED, the headline read. My parents' engagement announcement, I thought, until I started to read the article.

> Mr. and Mrs. George Alexander Sinclair announce the engagement of their daughter Katherine Anne to Mr. James Arthur Durbin of Cottonwood Falls, Washington . . .

Next to the article was a picture, not of Mom, but of Kathy. My aunt had been engaged to my father?

"What you got there?" Crystal asked. I hadn't heard her come back in the room.

"Nothing." I quickly closed the screen.

"Oh, it looks like something to me," Crystal said. "Come on. What is it?"

She clicked the screen open again and read the article, her mouth quickly forming the words, her eyes getting wider as she read.

"My God! She stole Kathy's fiancé!"

"We don't know that for sure," I said quickly. "Maybe Kathy broke it off. Maybe Mom was second choice."

"Oh, right," Crystal said. "Don't you see? He met Cindy and fell in love with her. He dropped your aunt and married your mom. That would explain a lot, wouldn't it?"

"Yeah. If it's true."

"It's true. I guarantee it."

At dinner that night Mom and I pretended that things were all right between us. Jimmy prattled on about Alonzo and Carlos and the kids at the Y. Before we went to bed, we both apologized for losing our tempers. And we meant it, but it didn't dissolve the tension. There were things we weren't telling each other, and we both knew it.

"We'll be out of here as soon as I can get my feet back under me," Mom said before she turned out the light. "School's going fine and I'll get a job soon."

I nodded. I knew she hated her classes, I knew she wasn't making very good grades, but I let her lie to me. What was one more little lie, anyway, in the ocean we were swimming in?

14

"That is so weird," Aspen said after he finished reading the printout of the engagement announcement. We were at the store, and a hard rain beat against the flat roof.

"Crystal thinks that's why Kathy acted the way she did at the house tour," I said.

"Makes sense," he said. "Are you going to ask your mother about it?"

"Are you kidding?"

"But she can't just blow it off."

"It's not worth it. Kathy isn't going to help us," I said. But I couldn't stop thinking about it. There was something creepy about the whole thing. Had my mother really stolen her sister's boyfriend and ruined her life? My mother, who was so judgmental of any social impropriety? It didn't seem like her at all. But somehow I knew it was.

It had been raining all day. Water poured through the

gutters and sprayed the sidewalk each time a car went by. The windows were misted over. When thunder cracked and the lights flickered, Aspen squeezed my hand.

"I doubt you'll get any business today," he said. "Got any new oil paints in the stockroom?" He leaned over the counter to kiss me, and my mood started to change.

"I think we do," I said as thunder rumbled again. "Just follow me."

The drumming rain seemed to fall even harder as we nestled ourselves in the tiny room that smelled faintly like paint but mostly like Aspen. I closed my eyes as his hands moved against my skin like a fine brush, painting me coral and rose. His tongue ran a clear silver line down my neck. Right now this was all that mattered, Aspen and the dark and the sound of rain.

Suddenly he pulled away.

"What's wrong?" I whispered.

"You hear something?" He leaned toward the door.

"No," I said. "Do you?"

"I think somebody is in the store. You'd better check."

"I didn't hear the bells—nobody's here." I pulled him toward me again and kissed him on the neck.

"You just didn't hear them over the storm," he said.

"Stop it. You're creeping me out."

"No really—listen."

We stood frozen in the dark, trying to hear over the drumming rain.

"Lucy?" Mom's voice was right outside the stockroom. And then she was pushing open the door. "What are you doing there in the dark?"

"Mom?" I shoved Aspen behind the door. This was not the time to introduce him to my mother. "I'm just getting supplies. The lights keep going out. . . ."

"Is someone in there with you?"

"Um . . . in here?"

"Yes, in there." She pushed the door open all the way, crushing Aspen against the wall. He let out a little yelp.

"It's just Aspen," I said. There was no way around it. "He works here sometimes."

"Hi," he said, stepping from behind the door. His cheeks were flushed. His shirt was hiked up on one side, but I didn't dare straighten it out. Mom was staring at him, taking in his dreadlocks, his eyebrow ring, his cannabis leaf T-shirt.

"I came by to see if you wanted a ride," she said, finally taking her eyes off him. "I didn't want you walking home in the rain."

"Thanks," I said. "But I've still got about fifteen minutes until closing."

"Yes, I know. I was going to wait for you," she said in that controlled voice that means she's really mad. "But with someone else here to lock up, you can come with me. Now."

"Actually, I can't lock up," Aspen said. "Linda doesn't trust me with the keys." He laughed nervously, then realized he'd said the wrong thing.

"I'll lock up," I blurted out. "You need to get going to that thing you need to be at, right?"

"Yeah, I've got to take off. For that thing. Nice to meet you," he told my mother, and hurried out into the rain.

. . .

"What is going on between the two of you?" Mom asked after we got back to St. Agatha's. She took off her wet raincoat and hung it over the chair. The whole drive home we had said nothing.

"We're just friends," I said.

"Let me ask you again, Lucy, and this time tell me the truth. What is going on between the two of you?"

"We hang out at school," I said, avoiding her eyes. "He comes by to see me at work sometimes."

"Comes by? I thought you said he worked there."

"He does, sort of." I tried to backtrack. "I mean, a couple times a week he straightens up the stockroom and stuff."

"Why can't you ever tell me the truth, Lucy?" she asked. "I'm not naive. Nobody cleans up in the dark."

"The lights went out!" I said.

"Lucy."

"Okay, we're kind of going out, I guess."

"Since when?" she asked.

"Not long."

"Specifically."

"Since February," I said.

"You've had a boyfriend since February? And you didn't tell me?" she said.

"Do you have to know every little detail of my personal life?" I asked. "And he's not a boyfriend."

"What do you call him, then?"

I didn't answer.

"I don't think a . . . boyfriend, whether you call him that or not, is a little detail. Especially if you feel like you have to keep him a secret." All of a sudden her expression changed. "He went to Seattle with you, didn't he? You spent the night with him in Ellensburg." How she suddenly had that revelation I don't know, but she was so sure of the fact that I couldn't even begin to deny it.

"It's not what you think," I said. "We had no idea we'd get stuck there."

"Did you sleep with him?"

"Mom!"

"Not that you'd tell me, anyway," she said. "I don't know what's happening to you, Lucy."

"What do you mean?"

"Well, look at him. He looks like . . . Well, he looks like a loser, frankly. And look at you lately," she said. "You used to care about your appearance. Now you just throw on anything, don't fix your hair, never wear makeup."

"I can't afford makeup!" I said. "And you're judging him without even knowing him. Just because he doesn't look like the boys at Bentley."

"It's more than that. All of a sudden you're running around with God knows who all, sneaking into motel rooms, leaving town without my permission. This is not how your father and I raised you."

"And you were perfect at my age?" I jerked Kathy's engagement announcement from my back pocket. "What's this all about, then? Is this why your only sister hates you?"

"Where did you get this?" she whispered.

"It doesn't matter where I got it. It's true, isn't it? We can't go to her for help because of what you did."

Mom opened her mouth, but said nothing. All the

anger seemed to drain out of her as she sat down heavily on the double bed. I felt drained too. And I wished I hadn't done things the way I had, throwing the article in her face. But she'd asked for it with her phony perfection crap and the way she'd treated Aspen.

"I'll tell you this story only once," Mom finally said. "After that I don't want you to ever ask me about it again, understand?"

I nodded and sat down across from her on the single bed.

"Kathy met your father her last year of college. After she graduated, she took a job here in Cottonwood Falls to be near him. I had just graduated from high school and I wanted to get away for the summer, so my parents decided I could come here and live with Kathy. I had just turned eighteen."

"So you met Dad while he was dating her?"

"They had become engaged right before I moved in. Your dad always said he and Kathy rushed into the engagement before they really knew each other. Your grandmother's sapphire? He had given her that as an engagement ring." She stopped and looked at me as if she expected me to say something. When I didn't, she went on. "For me it was love at first sight. Maybe it was for him too. But whatever it was, we didn't handle it very well."

"Didn't he tell her? I mean, once he knew he didn't—want to marry her anymore?" I asked. I found myself actually feeling kind of sorry for my aunt.

"Things weren't that simple. For a long time he couldn't decide. He'd take Kathy out at night while I was working as a waitress, and then during the day while she was at work, he'd come over to see me."

"Didn't he have a job? Somewhere he had to be all day?"

"He was working for a bank, in repossession. His hours were pretty much his own."

"So he was involved with both of you, then?" I said, trying to absorb it all. "And Kathy didn't know, but you did?"

"It was wrong. But back then it just seemed exciting. Kathy and I never really got along. We were always trying to outdo each other with school and friends and looks. So it was easy for me to make excuses. And I loved your father. I really did."

"But Dad was older," I said.

"You mean he should have known better? Maybe. But knowing something and doing it are very different things. One day she came home early."

"And she found you together."

Mom nodded. She wasn't going to tell me where Kathy found them, but I had a pretty good idea.

"I couldn't live with her anymore. And I couldn't go back home, so I moved in with him."

"You and Dad lived together?"

"For about a year. I didn't really know what else to do," Mom said. "We got married by the justice of the peace. I'd always dreamed of having a big wedding, but we couldn't after all that. My parents were hardly speaking to me. At that point I was just happy he was finally going to marry me." She sighed. "It's not something I'm proud of, Lucy.

Even though I loved your father, he was not always easy to be with."

I lay on the bed with my eyes closed, wishing I didn't know these things. Wishing my father had been the man I'd thought he was when he died. Not the philandering repo man who married my mother too young. Not the man who left us with nothing but memories that kept crumbling until they weren't even worth having.

I didn't expect to meet Aspen on the school steps the next morning, not after the way Mom had treated him at the store. But there he was, pouring me a cup of hot chocolate from his Thermos.

"You doing okay?" he asked, and handed me the cup.

"It's just my mom," I said. "I'm sorry about the way she acted."

Aspen shrugged. "I guess I surprised her."

"Yeah." I paused. "She knows all about Ellensburg."

"You're kidding. She knows about Motel Six and everything?"

I nodded. "But I think she's even more ticked off because she didn't know anything about you until yesterday."

"Not anything?" Aspen asked.

I hesitated. "I was afraid she wouldn't like you."

"Thanks. That makes me feel a lot better."

"I didn't mean it that way," I said. But how *did* I mean it? I had to admit that I'd never introduced Aspen to her, never even mentioned him, because he wouldn't measure up to her expectations. Did that mean I was somehow ashamed of him?

Aspen screwed the top on the Thermos. By the way he

held his mouth in a thin line, by the way his eyes moved restlessly, looking at everything but me, I could tell he was hurt. He expected me to say something, but what? I didn't want to talk about it. I wanted to be alone, but I stood there with him until the bell rang. For some reason I couldn't just walk away.

I sat through first period in a daze. Right before second period I checked myself out at the office, claiming I didn't feel well, which was true enough. Instead of heading back toward St. Agatha's, I caught a city bus going in the opposite direction, up the South Hill through suburbs and parks. At the end of the line I got off and walked another mile through the familiar neighborhood of Andover Hills, until I reached our house.

Not that it was ours anymore. The mortgage company had taken possession of it months ago. A FOR SALE sign stood in the front yard. I peered through the windows at the empty rooms, at the granite countertops, at the doorknobs and light fixtures that Mom had spent so much time picking out. At the impressions left in the carpet by the heavy entertainment center that Circuit City had repossessed. Ironic for my dad, the former repo man, to have it all taken away.

In the far corner of the backyard stood the wooden swing set Dad had put up for Jimmy just last spring. I sat down on one of the swings, remembering how Dad and his friend Andy had spent a whole weekend working on it. Mom had interrupted them every couple of hours with trays of food and iced tea. After they were finished, Andy and Dad had sipped beers on the deck.

That afternoon my dad had sat there looking like any other father. But there were secrets, so many secrets. And lies about money and love. What had Mom meant when she said he wasn't easy to be with? Was there something else that I didn't know about? When I closed my eyes, I could see him on the deck, turning up his bottle of beer, laughing at something Andy said.

How could you have taken so much and left so little? I silently asked him. He raised his bottle to me, but he didn't answer.

I caught the bus back to Randolf before lunch was over. Aspen was in the art room with some of his friends.

"Where were you second period?" he asked, his voice both accusing and worried. "I thought maybe you went home."

"I did," I said. "But now I'm back."

15

"Have you seen the new girl?" Crystal asked when I got home that afternoon. She was in the kitchen with Jan and Ruthanne, feeding Chelsea Rose a bowl of mushy beige stuff. Chelsea Rose was plastering it across her forehead with no intention of putting any of it into her mouth.

"She's Romanian," Jan said, handing me a bowl of popcorn she had just made. "Can't speak a lick of English."

"But she looks like a model," Crystal said.

"Except she's at least six months pregnant," Ruthanne added.

"She was one of those Internet brides," Crystal said in a low voice.

"You don't know that for sure," Jan said. "That's just what Tina told you, and you can't trust her as far as you can throw her."

"Ruthanne heard it too," Crystal said, and Ruthanne nodded.

"What's an Internet bride?" I asked.

"These agencies advertise women, and then a man can pay a delivery fee and she's his," Ruthanne explained.

"That is totally weird!" I said. "You make it sound like ordering sports equipment."

"It is, considering that most men expect a daily workout from the shipment."

"But who would do that?" I asked.

"What man wouldn't?" Jan asked. "Get some exotic woman who can't talk back. At least not in English."

"I mean, what woman would sign up for that kind of thing?"

"One who wants to come to America, see *Oprah*, shop at Wal-Mart," Crystal said. "Where have you been, Lucy?"

Jan shushed us, and we tried not to stare at the tall, dark pregnant woman who had just walked into the room. I could see what Crystal meant about her being model material. She was easily one of the most beautiful women I'd ever seen. My fingers itched for a pencil and paper. Jan picked up the bowl of popcorn and went over to her.

"Hi. I'm Jan," she said in a loud slow voice, as if the woman were deaf, not foreign. "You want popcorn?"

The woman looked at her through wispy black bangs. Her eyes were dark bluish gray, almost lavender. She seemed puzzled until Jan shook the bowl at her, and she took a handful of popcorn.

Jan pointed to herself and said her name loudly.

"Tatyana," the woman said, and pointed to herself. Her voice was low and musical.

Taking her elbow, Jan led her over to the table where we sat. "This is Tatyana," she said, pronouncing it almost right. Then she pointed at the rest of us. "Crystal and Chelsea Rose. Ruthanne and Lucy."

Ruthanne gave a little wave. Tatyana smiled shyly. Then she took another handful of popcorn and floated out of the room.

"You think she'll ever learn English?" Ruthanne asked.

"People can learn just about anything they set their mind to," Jan said.

"Well, she isn't all that friendly," Crystal said.

"Give her time," Jan said. "You weren't all that friendly either at first."

I was about to mention my first morning at St. Agatha's and the milk carton, when Jimmy dashed into the kitchen.

"How's it going, J-man?" Crystal gave him a high five. He laughed at Chelsea Rose's messy face and tickled her under the chin. Then he turned to me.

"You got to come upstairs," he said, getting serious. "Mom's kind of mad about something."

"What's she mad about?" I asked, though I could name a number of possibilities.

"I don't know. Just come on," he said.

Crystal and I exchanged glances. I had told her about the blowup over Aspen and the conversation about Kathy that had followed. I'd left out some of the details, but she pretty much knew the whole story.

"Come with me, Jimbo, and we'll find Carlos," she said.

Mom sat in the chair by the window staring at a sheet of paper.

"What's wrong?" I asked.

"I flunked. We got our quarter grades today." She handed me the grade report: three Ds and an F.

"You didn't flunk. You've still got a grade point."

"Below a one!" she exclaimed.

"You'll do better next quarter," I said.

She shook her head. "Even if I did, I hate this stuff. The last thing I want to do with my life is sit in a cubicle with my fingers on a keyboard."

"So, what *do* you want to do?"

"What I'd been doing for sixteen years." She wiped her nose. "Having a family, keeping a house. That's the only thing I've ever wanted to do. It's the only thing I've ever done well."

"That's because you haven't found the right profession," I said, trying to sound optimistic. "I'm sure there's something else you're good at."

"But what? I just want to get us out of here."

"We will get out," I said, fighting the sinking feeling in my chest. "It just might take a little longer than we thought."

She carefully folded the grade report and put it inside her math book. "I think I'll lie down for a while," she said. "Would you turn out the light before you leave?"

I closed the door quietly behind me and went down to the courtyard. It was a nice afternoon, the first one all year. The remnants of dirty snow had finally melted, and the air felt almost like spring. Crystal was sitting on top of one of the picnic tables that had recently been hauled out of storage.

"Everything okay?" she asked.

"She flunked math," I said.

"That sucks," she said. "But look at it this way. Your mom only failed a math class. She didn't fail a drug rehab program. She didn't break probation or go back on the streets. She's not in jail for beating her kids."

"I know," I said.

"Alls I'm saying is, it could be a hell of a lot worse."

Or a hell of a lot better, I thought.

16

For the first time since we'd moved in, life at St. Agatha's began to feel frighteningly permanent. The dream of being saved by Kathy had turned into a nightmare. Mom's plan to get her degree and land a good job seemed as silly as Alonzo's plan to own a fire truck. I began to understand how Jan could still be living in the shelter after more than a year, how Crystal, as much as she hated it, saw it as an indefinite waiting place. It's not forever, she would say, but it seemed to me that the longer we stayed, the more dependent we became, like we were addicted to failure.

I worked as much as I could. Mom agreed to let me pick up a couple of extra hours on Saturday mornings. Despite any fears she might have had about me having sex in the stockroom, the money was too important to pass up. I also began putting more effort into my schoolwork. The only way I could go to college was to pay for it myself, and that meant getting scholarships.

"I've got a huge test on *The Odyssey* tomorrow," I told Aspen one afternoon. He still came by the store, but less frequently now. I got the feeling he was still kind of mad at me for not letting Mom know he existed.

"So?" he pulled on the belt loop of my jeans.

"So would you quit tugging on me?"

"You want me to leave?" he asked, surprised by the irritation in my voice. I was a little surprised myself.

"I didn't say that."

"Well, that's what it sounded like." He crossed his arms.

"I just can't afford to be distracted right now," I said.

"Oh, so I'm a distraction."

"What is your problem?" I said. "I've got to ace this test."

"It's not *my* problem, Lucy," he said. "I don't have a problem."

"Meaning . . ."

"Meaning lately you've been acting really different. What's up, anyway?"

I didn't answer. What could I say? I was acting different, but only because everything *was* different—how I felt about work and school and my family. Even how I felt about him. Did I really have time for him right now?

"Is your mother still giving you crap?" he asked. "Or is it just me?"

"Maybe we should stop seeing so much of each other," I said. It wasn't what I'd planned to say, but there it was.

The words hung in the air like a cold fog. Aspen seemed to flinch against the chill; then his face settled into an indifferent expression.

"You're probably right," he said.

I nodded, unable to meet his eyes. "That doesn't mean we can't still be friends."

"Oh, sure, we'll still be friends," he said with a thin, stiff smile. "I'll let you get back to your studying. See you around."

The bells jangled as he walked out the door, and I felt emptied out, hollow, but also relieved. Now I could simplify my life, focus on my grades, on making money, on getting Mom on track and headed out of the shelter.

Aspen had been taking up way too much of my attention.

"What's got you so bummed lately?" Crystal asked one night after dinner. Her kitchen timer had just gone off. She closed her science book and was ready to talk, even though I was still trying to study.

"I'm just a little stressed about school," I said without looking up from my Spanish book, hoping she'd take the hint.

"Wrong answer. It's Aspen, isn't it?" she said. "Elton said you two don't hang around like you used to. Did you break up?"

"Technically we weren't ever going out, so how could we break up?"

"What would you call it?" she persisted. "You didn't break up, but you're not together anymore."

"I don't know."

"But it sucks, doesn't it?" She narrowed her eyes at me. "Tell the truth. Doesn't it?"

I chose not to answer. I didn't want to admit to Crystal that I missed Aspen. I didn't even want to admit it to myself. It had been two weeks since he'd last come into the store. Not that I expected him to, but I did expect him to at least speak to me at school. At the same time I didn't want to waste my time with him anymore. I missed having him around, but needed to be alone. Seeing him always put me in a bad mood, but if he wasn't in second period, I couldn't stop wondering where he was.

And lately he'd started hanging out with that girl named Mariah, the queen of the flower children. She was really pretty, tall, thin, beautifully pale. Her black hair hung to her waist and her eyes were emerald green.

"Contacts," Elton told me. "The tinted kind."

We were eating lunch at Michelangelo's, and I couldn't help asking about her. She and Aspen had been sitting on the front steps, and we'd walked right past them on our way to lunch. Mariah was practically sitting in his lap, and Aspen was brushing the end of her long black braid against his cheek. Elton stopped to say hi to them, but I kept going down the steps. I felt like throwing up.

"In middle school she had glasses and short hair," Elton continued. "She was kind of nerdy back then."

"So, have she and Aspen known each other long?" I couldn't get the image of Aspen's hand woven in her braid out of my mind.

"I don't know how long, but they went out last year."

"She was his girlfriend?"

"They ate lunch together. They hung out after school, stuff like that." Stuff like that was what Aspen had been doing with me until about two weeks ago.

"I guess they're back together, then," I said, trying to sound unconcerned.

"Does that bother you?" Elton asked.

"Why should it?" I said. "He can have a girlfriend if he wants to." Only two weeks ago Aspen was kissing me in the stockroom. I guess now he was hooking up with Mariah instead.

As we walked back to Randolf and the second half of the school day, Elton invited me to come hear his band at the Yellow Door with Crystal on Saturday night.

"Jan's going to babysit Chelsea Rose," he said. "I'd pick you guys up, but I've got to be there early to set up. Crystal usually takes the bus. Come with her."

"I don't know," I said, considering the money, always my first thought, then thinking about what Mom would say.

"I'll put you on the guest list," he said. "Just in case."

17

"Don't you think she's kind of bizarre?" Crystal asked Mom. They were washing windows with Jan and talking about Tatyana.

"I'm sure this is a complete shock to her," Mom said sternly. "She can barely communicate with anyone. She's totally alone, and I doubt she's even twenty years old. She's probably scared to death." Mom's response took me by surprise. In the months we'd been at St. Agatha's she had shown little interest in anyone but Jan and Crystal, and that was only because I'd gotten to know them first. Now here she was taking up for a total stranger.

"Anyway, Rachel's looking for somebody to be Tatyana's doula," Crystal said. "Jan was mine." She punched Jan gently in the arm and smiled at her.

"What's a doula?" I asked.

"You don't know anything, do you?" Crystal gloated. Knowing more than I did always put her in a good mood. "She's like a mentor. First she goes to childbirth classes with you and she's there when the baby comes. And then she mentors you on how to take care of the baby."

"Crystal was a natural mother. I didn't have much to do," Jan said.

"Yeah, but if you hadn't been there, I never would have been able to stand it. I wanted Elton, but his parents had decided to take a family vacation the week of my due date. Very convenient. For them at least."

"I could do that," Mom said suddenly.

"Do what?" I asked.

"Be Tatyana's doula. Why not? I've had babies. I was even good at it." She put down her bottle of Windex and went straight into the office to talk to Rachel before I could say a word.

"Don't you think you ought to be focusing on school instead of Tatyana's birthing classes?" I asked later that night. This sudden interest in Tatyana at the expense of getting us out of St. Agatha's was worrying me.

"I need something else," she said.

What about us? I wanted to ask. What about Jimmy? He seemed to zigzag between toddlerhood and Mr. J-man, the five-year-old smart-ass.

"And more importantly, Tatyana needs someone," Mom went on. "Rachel said she's been in the U.S. less than a year. She was married to a man she'd never laid eyes on until she got off the plane. She literally had to escape through the bathroom window of his apartment. But all that's confidential information," she added.

"Nothing at St. Agatha's is confidential," I reminded her. "When does she start these classes?"

"Next week," Mom said. She sat there twirling her pencil for a minute. "Look, I can tell you think this is a bad idea, but it's something I need to do."

"But why?"

"All we have here is a room and a corner of a kitchen. This gives me space, in a way. Do you understand?"

I shrugged. It seemed to me Mom was looking for distractions. From school, from living here, from getting us out. By taking care of Tatyana she was ignoring so much else, but I couldn't tell her that. She was the grown-up. She ought to be able to figure it out for herself.

Whatever Crystal told Mom about going to the Yellow Door worked. When I asked Crystal what she'd said, she started singing, "Girls Just Want to Have Fun," and reminded me she could be very persuasive.

"But what *did* you say? Specifically," I nagged. We were sitting in the back of an almost empty bus.

"I told her you'd be back at eleven. I told her you'd check in with her. You can use Elton's cell. I reminded her that the Yellow Door is not a bar but an all-ages club."

"I could have told her all that and it wouldn't have mattered," I said.

"Frankly, I think she's kind of worried about you."

"About what?" I asked. "That I'll find another suspicious-looking guy to hang out with?"

"No. She's worried about all work and no play. And no friends to speak of. She thinks you're missing out on the so-called best years of your life."

"If these are the best years of my life, shoot me," I said. "Besides, I have friends."

"Name some. Besides me, I mean."

"Jan. Elton."

"And Aspen. Except you screwed that up," Crystal said.

"Would you just shut up about Aspen?" I said. Ever since we'd broken up or whatever, she'd been giving me grief. Like it was my fault. "You just don't understand. I don't have time for a guy right now. I can't have all these demands on me."

"Whatever," Crystal said, and stood up as the bus slowed at the curb. "This is our stop. Get ready to rock and roll."

The Yellow Door had been an empty warehouse before its owner put in a stage and a sound system and opened it up to local bands. It was popular with high school kids, who couldn't get into regular clubs, but college students hung out there too. When we got there it was already packed. We gave our names at the door and got purple stamps on our hands. Crystal grabbed my arm, and we made our way to a table where Elton sat with his band.

"Meet Bogus Orange," she said, and introduced me to four twenty-something guys. Elton found two more chairs, and I sat down feeling nervous and young.

"What do you want to drink?" Elton asked, and Crystal sent him to the bar for two Cokes.

"You want to come up for 'Desperate Measures'?" a guy with a braided goatee asked Crystal.

"Sure. As long as it's before ten-thirty," she said. "I got to pick up Chelsea Rose from the sitter by eleven." I silently thanked her for not giving the real reason for having to leave so early, that I had a curfew.

"You got it," the guy said as the band headed toward the stage. He nodded to me. "See you later."

"You're singing?" I asked Crystal as the band took their places. "Onstage?"

"Where else? You make it sound like a big deal." Crystal laughed. "I used to sing with the band all the time. Then I got pregnant and it didn't look right having this blimp on the stage with all these hot guys. Don't you think they're hot?"

"Yeah, I guess. Maybe the blond one."

"David? I could introduce you."

"You did," I said.

"You know what I mean," Crystal said. "David's single. He's a nice guy."

I shook my head. "I don't have time—"

"I know, I know. But I don't believe you."

Once the band started playing, it was hard to talk. It had been ages since I'd been out, and I'd never been to a place quite like the Yellow Door. My old friends hung out playing pool in the basements of each other's big houses or at someone's ski condo. They moved in a world of designer clothes and tennis lessons and spring break in Los Cabos. The crowd at the Yellow Door made Aspen look ordinary. Most of them were pierced, tattooed and dyed multiple times. And their clothes—you'd never find those at the mall. Bogus Orange had a unique sound that I liked a lot. Crystal described it as percussion-based metal with a twist of punk. Whatever. It sounded good to me.

I was getting into the music when Crystal suddenly elbowed me, nearly upsetting my soda.

"Don't look now," she shouted in my ear. So of course I looked, and there just inside the door stood Aspen and Mariah. They were holding hands.

"Shit," Crystal said. "They would have to come here."

"It's okay," I said, and involuntarily put my hand to my chest. "I'm all right."

"No you're not. You look like you just witnessed a natural disaster."

Aspen glanced at us and looked surprised to see me. When he caught himself staring, he waved.

"He can't be coming over here," Crystal said. But he was. After saying something to Mariah, he wove his way through the crowd to our table. She watched him with an amused expression on her face—was she laughing at me?

"I didn't expect to see you two here," he said, smiling.

"Why not?" Crystal snapped. I stared down at the table.

"I don't know. I just didn't," he said. "So, how are things going?" he asked me.

"Okay."

He stood there a minute, then glanced back at Mariah, who was waiting at the bar. "Well, I guess I better go."

"Yeah," I said.

"Why didn't you talk to him?" Crystal punched me

in the arm as Aspen made his way back through the crowded room.

"Ow! That hurt." I rubbed my arm. "What was I supposed to say?"

"Words would have been good."

"Well, you didn't help much, being so snippy."

"Why shouldn't he expect to see us here? We can go wherever we want to."

I didn't feel like shouting over the music, so I just shrugged. I sat with my back to the bar, wanting to watch Aspen but not wanting to see him with Mariah. If I'd never met him, my life would have been so much easier now.

When the song ended, Elton motioned to Crystal. She took a rhinestone tiara out of her bag and placed it on her head.

"Is it straight?" she asked.

"You're going to wear that?" I laughed.

"Of course. It's my trademark." As she headed toward the stage, David, the cute blond guy, shouted into the mike, "Give a warm welcome to Bogus Orange's own Queen of Rock! Crystal Brick!" The crowd went nuts. And then she was onstage and the band was playing and she was singing, her deep warm voice carrying strong and clear over the drums and guitars.

> I can't stand to see you
> I can't see without you
> The space where you touched me
> Is numb, it's gone.

And I'm left in measureless depths
And I'm left taking desperate measures.

I sat alone, letting her voice pull at the empty spot between my ribs. Finally I turned toward the bar to see where Aspen was. But he and Mariah were gone.

When we got back to St. Agatha's, I checked in with Mom while Crystal picked up Chelsea Rose from Jan. Then we went back to her room.

"You know, you could still make it work out," she said. "I could see him from the stage. He was looking straight at you."

"He left, didn't he? Obviously me being there didn't matter."

"It probably mattered a lot. Don't you see, he didn't want to hang around because it was too hard to see you."

"He was with someone else, Crystal. He left because he was with her."

"The way he is with Mariah is nothing like the way he was with you," she said. "They just stood there. They didn't talk or laugh. I can tell when two people are bored with each other."

"Okay. Even if I did believe you, what would be the point?"

"Dammit, Lucy! That's your main problem. Not everything in life has a point. Some things just are what they are."

I was wide awake before daybreak. Taking my sketchbook, I went downstairs and curled up on a couch. I drew what I had been dreaming: a stone tower, long black hair like Rapunzel's, someone drowning as the hair became a moat at the tower's base. A hand holding water, which became hair again, braided and as soft as a feather against someone's cheek.

18

"Maybe you should try retail," Crystal was saying to Mom as I came into the kitchen later that morning. They were wiping down the counters with 409. "I bet you'd be good at selling things."

"How about real estate?" Jan suggested. "You watched your husband build houses for years." She squeezed a sponge into the sink, then sat down at the table where Tatyana was knitting. Several days ago someone had donated a couple of bags of yarn skeins. Though the colors weren't exactly infant-friendly, Tatyana was going through the yarn at an amazing rate. Right now she was making a tiny burgundy and gray striped sweater. Jimmy, Alonzo and Carlos were at another table building houses with LEGOs.

Classes at the community college would start the next morning, and Mom still hadn't registered. She had three days before registration closed. Then she'd have to wait twelve more weeks for the next quarter. If she didn't think of something fast, it would be late summer before she even got started.

"Do what you do most good," Tatyana suggested as she finished off the little sweater.

"Which is?" Crystal asked.

"Make food to eat." For a moment no one said anything.

"You mean work in a restaurant?" Mom asked. Tatyana shrugged, maybe not understanding the word *restaurant*, and began knitting a pair of booties out of black yarn.

"Of course in a restaurant," Jan said, and threw her arm around Tatyana's shoulder. "Girl, you've found the answer."

Tatyana ducked her head shyly and grinned, fingers flying.

"They got food service classes at CFCC, in their— what's it called—their culinary arts institute," Jan said. "All you got to do is sign up for them, Cindy."

We all sat there, stunned by the obvious, wondering why no one had thought of it before.

"But I couldn't cook for paying customers," Mom protested.

"You don't know until you try," Jan said. "Look at me. I didn't think I'd ever get clean, but here I am. Got my boy back. Got my GED. I'll be certified in another quarter. And look at Crystal here."

"Plus you don't have to work in a restaurant. There must be lots of things you could do with a food services degree," I said, suddenly excited by the idea.

"Yeah," Crystal said. "You could be a lunch lady at the middle school."

Mom looked horrified until she realized Crystal was joking. "I'd have to stock up on hairnets!" she said, laughing.

"And white uniforms," I said.

"And those shoes like giant marshmallows," Crystal added.

Mom and Jan were laughing at the thought of serving mystery meat. And Tatyana was laughing at them. Crystal looked at me, and we burst into giggles. Overcome with silliness and relief, I didn't notice Tina. Suddenly there she was, standing beside the table.

"Tina," Jan said. "Pull up a chair and join us."

"They stole my car," Tina said. Crystal and Jan exchanged glances while Mom looked down at her hands.

"You don't have a car," Jan reminded her gently. Tatyana looked at her curiously. Her stare seemed to make Tina angry.

"She stole it," Tina said, pointing at Tatyana.

"She didn't steal your car, Tina." Jan stood up as Tina took a step forward. "You totaled it months ago, remember?"

Tina looked confused.

"Rachel wants to talk to you," Jan said, taking her by the arm.

"Has Rachel got my car?"

"I don't know, Tina. Let's go see."

"She's getting worse," Crystal said in a low voice as Jan led Tina out of the kitchen. "I heard her about three this morning yelling at Alonzo. Jan took him to her room while I went for Paula."

"She needs help," Mom said, and glanced at Alonzo. He'd waved as Tina left the room, but she'd looked right through him. "It can't be good for him."

"Yeah, I don't think the outpatient thing is working so well. I heard Rachel on the phone with her therapist and—"

"Don't tell us," Mom said, and held up her hand.

Jan returned from the office. "I think I'll take the boys down to the park. Get them out of the way. Can Jimbo come along?" she asked Mom.

Mom hesitated. She was worried about Tina following them.

"They'll be fine with Jan," I said. "Rachel won't let Tina out when she's like this."

"I just wish there was something they could do for her," Mom said. Tatyana nodded, understanding the situation even if she didn't understand all of the words.

When I got home from work Monday afternoon, Mom was full of news about the community college's Culinary Arts Center.

"They've got everything from food sanitation to modern cuisine," she said, showing me the course catalog. "Advanced desserts, banquet, East Indian cuisine . . ."

"What did you sign up for?" I asked.

"Roger suggested restaurant management, advanced desserts and modern cuisine."

"Roger?"

"My advisor," she said, and I could have sworn she was blushing.

Every day she came home chattering like a squirrel. You'd think food services was the most interesting profession available to humankind. Even Jan's eyes glazed over a couple of times as Mom went on about presentation and sanitation. But I was happy for her. She seemed more like her old self than she had since my birthday. She talked about how amazing it was to use professional cookware and how nice the other students were. Roger's name came up too.

"So what's up with this Roger guy, anyway?" I asked one night. I was cleaning up after coq au vin made with nonalcoholic wine. Dinner had been fabulous. We'd had chocolate mousse, one of her assignments, and Mom was in a great mood.

"I already told you, he's my academic advisor," she said.

"Yeah, I know. But you seem to be seeing an awful lot of him."

"I guess I need an awful lot of advice," she said.

"How old is he?"

"Heavens, Lucy, I don't know."

"Make an estimate," I said.

"Forty-five, maybe fifty."

"Married?"

"Divorced. I know what you're thinking," Mom said. "But Roger is very kind. I appreciate his help."

"Okay. Subject closed," I said. But I could tell by the way she couldn't stop smiling that Roger was interested in more than her career path.

How did I feel about that? How should I feel?

It had been only nine months since Dad died, but it seemed like years. We had moved three times, if you counted the motel. Jimmy had grown incredibly fast, both in size and independence. I had gotten a job, fallen in and out of love (or something), made new friends. The world was a totally different place. Maybe I should have been more loyal to my father's memory, but I was beginning to understand that memories were only stories about how things used to be. Or how we wished they used to be. They had no more connection to what was happening now than fairy tales.

19

When the fire alarm went off about three-thirty, I sat up in bed, thinking that the system was malfunctioning like it had the night after my birthday. Mom thought the same thing, but she turned on the bedside lamp and slipped on her robe and shoes. Fire or no fire, we'd have to evacuate.

"Do you smell smoke?" Mom asked suddenly. I was helping Jimmy get his shoes on. I sniffed the air. After a second I could smell it too.

"My God, this time it's real," I said, and adrenaline shot through me like ice water. Remembering something I had learned in elementary school, I put my hand against the door to the hallway. It felt cool, so I opened it. The alarm sounded much louder with the door open, and I put my hands over my ears. Thin smoke drifted in the air.

"I think it's down at the other end of the hall," I shouted over the alarm. Several other doors opened, and people started hurrying toward the stairs. The smoke was getting thicker, so I dumped the glass of water I kept by my bed on Jimmy's T-shirt and pulled the shirt up over his nose.

"What are you doing?" he yelled at me.

"Keep your face covered," I said. "And bend over like this." Mom took Jimmy's hand, and as we moved down the hall, we knocked on closed doors, trying to rouse anyone who might still be sleeping. Already we could hear sirens heading along Regal Park for St. Agatha's.

When we got outside, a police car pulled up and officers began directing us away from the building. Paula was talking to Rachel on her cell phone and counting residents at the same time. Women were calling to each other and holding their children close. The police car's headlights cast strange shadows as people hurried in front of them.

Suddenly bright orange flames shot out of one of the second-floor windows.

"That's Tina's room!" Jan said. She told Carlos to stay with Mom and started searching frantically through the crowd for Alonzo and Tina.

"Where's Tatyana?" Mom shouted.

"Over there." I waved my arms at her. Clutching a large plastic bag full of tiny knitted clothes, she hurried over to us. She was talking fast in Romanian and holding the bag so tight it might have been the baby itself.

Crystal ran up to us, holding Chelsea Rose against her

shoulder. Chelsea Rose's eyes were as big as quarters, but she didn't cry. We stood close together and watched the flames in the window get redder and higher.

"It's Tina's room, isn't it?" Crystal asked, though she knew it was. Tina's room was the room right next to hers.

"Yeah. Have you seen her and Alonzo?"

Crystal shook her head and put her arm around Carlos. "I hope to God they're okay."

We watched the fire lick the roof of St. Agatha's, and then Carlos let out a yell.

"There he is. There comes Lonzo now!" Carlos pointed to the window next to the one shooting flames. Alonzo was straddling the windowsill and rubbing his eyes.

"Do you think he'll try to jump?" I asked. Mom pressed Jimmy's face against her so he couldn't watch whatever was about to happen. Crystal stepped in front of Carlos to block his view.

Everyone was shouting at Alonzo not to move. He looked so small against the glaring light, like he might blow away into the darkness. A firefighter leaned an aluminum ladder against the roof.

"His mama might be in there too!" Jan shouted at a police officer.

"If there's anyone else up there, we'll find them," he shouted back.

The firefighter on the ladder reached the window and helped Alonzo onto his back. As they started down, there was hardly a sound from the women and children waiting across the street. Even the babies seemed to hold their breaths. When they reached the bottom, Jan ran across the street and grabbed Alonzo, and we all started cheering. Alonzo was crying and coughing and holding tight around Jan's neck. But he was all right.

"Mama's still in there," he gasped. "She said she was gonna get me a fire truck. She lit a match to the paper and said I could have a red fire truck. I told her not to," he cried.

Jan shushed him. "They'll get her out," she said. "You just don't talk anymore, okay?"

"Damn that Tina," Crystal said in a low voice. "Damn her if they don't get her out, and I'll kill her if they do."

We watched the water shooting high against the walls of St. Agatha's. In a few minutes two medics hurried from the back of the building to a waiting ambulance. They carried someone on a stretcher. We all knew who it was.

By midmorning things had settled down and the Red Cross was passing out sandwiches, bottled water and blankets. Television cameras were pointed at the St. Agatha's residents, and newscasters were interviewing anyone they could. Mom refused to talk to them, and I followed her lead. This was the biggest news to hit Cottonwood Falls in some time, but I wished they'd just go away. Although the Red Cross had set up a shelter in the Methodist church nearby, most of the women and children were still milling around in their pajamas, hoping for a chance to go back in and at least get some clothes. The rumor was out that Tina had started the fire, and people were remembering earlier false alarms and telling stories about her strange behavior.

"You'd think they'd leave the poor woman alone," Jan said. "Being in the hospital with burns all over her arms ought to be enough, but they got to go and rake her over the coals some more." We were sitting on blankets holding bologna sandwiches that nobody felt like eating. The whole scene looked like some demented picnic.

"Where we will sleep?" Tatyana asked Mom. She had pulled some yarn and a crochet hook out of her bag and was starting on a mustard-gold receiving blanket.

"Rachel and Paula will tell us what to do. Don't worry," Mom said, pretending not to be worried herself.

Jimmy and Carlos had gathered some empty cardboard boxes from the Red Cross station. They stacked the boxes to make walls, then pulled a blanket over the top. Carlos got on his hands and knees and stuck his head through the cardboard shelter's door.

"It's too little for me," he said, wrinkling his forehead.

Jimmy carefully wedged his shoulders between the boxes, then backed out again. "Yeah, for me too," he said. Then he turned to Crystal. "Can Chelsea come in?"

Crystal put Chelsea Rose on the grass, and she crawled into the boys' little house.

"It's a baby house," Jimmy said, and laughed. "Just her size."

Inside the house Chelsea Rose sat up and clapped.

Crystal adjusted the blanket roof. "Now if the rest of us can just find a place . . ." She gazed off down the street as if she heard a familiar voice calling her.

"Isn't that Elton's car?" I asked, but she was already running across the parking lot. Elton's noisy black Subaru pulled up to the curb, and he climbed out and hugged her. Chelsea started to crawl after her mother. I picked her up and bounced her on my hip so she wouldn't cry.

At first I didn't notice someone else getting out of the car. It was Aspen. Without thinking, I handed Chelsea to Jan and started walking toward him. He stood beside the open door for a minute, then came over.

"Elton called me as soon as he heard," he said. "Are you okay?"

"I'm fine," I said, pulling the brown Red Cross blanket tight over my pajamas.

"How did it start?" he asked.

"They're not sure yet," I said. I didn't want to mention Tina.

We stared at the blackened wall of St. Agatha's for a few seconds, not saying anything, not knowing what to say. I was surprised to see him, surprised at how glad I was he had come.

"Look, do you want to come over to my house? Ann said she would be more than happy to have you guys hang out until you've got someplace to go."

I looked back at Mom. She had stood up and was straightening her bathrobe. "I don't know."

"You could shower," Aspen added. "I'm sure we could find some clothes for you to borrow. And your mom and Jimmy too. Whoever needs a place."

"I'll tell her," I said. "Can you wait a second?"

"Sure," he said. "We have lots of room."

"Aspen's mom asked us to come over until we can get back in," I said. The whole time I had been talking to Aspen, Mom had pretended to be looking at something else. Now she pretended to be surprised to see him standing near Elton's car.

"I don't think we need to do that," she said.

"Why not?"

"We should wait until we can get inside and see about things," she said. But I knew she was embarrassed about how she had treated him, about what she had thought of him.

"They're not going to let us back in, Mom. Not anytime soon."

"I'm sure Rachel and Paula are making arrangements," Mom said.

"At the Methodist church!" I said. "We'll be sleeping on cots." I'd seen those shelters on TV, cots lined up not a foot apart, wall-to-wall misery. I'd sleep in the park before I slept in one of those places.

"We don't know them, Lucy. We can't just barge in."

"I know them," I said, and grabbed Jimmy by the hand. "That's where I'm staying, and Jimmy's coming with me. You can do what you want."

Mom looked at Tatyana clutching her bag of baby clothes. "All right," she said. "We'll all go, but only until we find somewhere else."

We spent most of the afternoon sitting in the wooden rocking chairs that lined Aspen's front porch. The late-April breeze was a little chilly, but we all wanted sun and fresh air. Mom was totally nervous at first, tangling her fingers together and smiling too hard. But once she realized how nice Ann was—and how normal for the mother of such a scary-looking kid—she relaxed. Ann found Mom and me something to wear. Tatyana ended up in a bright orange kaftan that Ann had bought in Morocco twenty years ago. One of those purchases that seemed perfect at the time, she said, shaking her head. She'd never worn it herself. Jimmy had on one of Aspen's T-shirts. It hung down to his knees.

"Like a dress," he said, scowling.

"No, like a knight's tunic," Aspen said, and buckled a wide leather belt around Jimmy's waist. Picking up a short stick, he tapped Jimmy on both shoulders.

"I knight thee Sir James," he said, and then presented it to him. Stick in hand, Jimmy ran around the front yard with Aspen's white dog, Bobby. Now that he knew Alonzo was safe, Jimmy seemed to regard the fire as an adventure, not a catastrophe. He wailed like a siren and told Aspen and Ann how the firefighter had rescued Alonzo.

"They can get over things quickly when they're little, as long as they have someone to talk to," Ann said.

"I hope you're right," Mom said. "It was terrifying to watch."

"Hey, Aspen, is that tree house back there yours?" Jimmy yelled as he raced around the corner of the house.

"You want to see it?" Aspen jumped off the porch. I could imagine him at ten or eleven in baggy shorts and giant sneakers.

"Aspen used to spend hours up there by himself," Ann said. "I worried about too much time alone, especially right after the divorce, but now I think it was important for him to have his own space."

"Ever since we moved to St. Agatha's, Jimmy has been obsessed with building make-believe houses," I said.

"It sounds like a healthy coping mechanism to me," Ann said, and Mom looked reassured.

• • •

That night Mom and Tatyana helped Ann make dinner. Jimmy had fallen asleep in front of the TV. I was dead tired myself, but every time I caught Aspen looking at me, I tingled with energy.

"Do you want to see the tree house?" he asked, brushing my hand with his long fingers. I followed him across the backyard to a large sycamore tree.

"Be careful, some of the ladder rungs are a little weak," he warned as he climbed the tree in front of me. The sun had warmed the bleached plywood walls. Purple maple leaves unfurled through the wide windows. The tree house smelled like leaves and sunshine.

"I used to come up here all the time," Aspen said as we sat down in a patch of light. "I even slept up here in the summers. I had a star chart, and I'd sit out here trying to discover new planets."

"Did you ever have friends sleep over?" I asked, remembering middle-school sleepovers—a dozen girls giving each other pedicures and watching movies in the basement.

"Yeah. Elton stayed over some. Back when we used to skate and stuff." He leaned back on his elbows and pointed through a gap in the leaves. "See that nest up there?"

I leaned back and tried.

"Look at that third branch up." He scooted over, and my chin grazed his shoulder. "It's a crow's nest. They come back to it every year to lay their eggs."

"The same ones?"

"Probably not the very same, but the chicks might

return as adults. I don't know for sure, but I like to think so."

"Crows are smart," I said, remembering the afternoon Aspen had told me he'd like to be a bird. "They use tools and solve problems, right?"

"And they're very gregarious. Did you know they hold funerals?"

"I know they move in flocks," I said.

"A flock is called a murder," Aspen said.

"Weird. You'd never see a murder of hawks." He had said I was like a hawk, alone, observant, a bird without a song, and I wondered if he was thinking the same thing now.

"But they pair up and stay together, hawks do. Sometimes," he said. We looked up at the crow's nest, our heads touching.

"It's not what you think," he said after a minute.

"What's not?" I asked, but I knew he was talking about Mariah.

"She's just a friend. She's actually got a boyfriend in college." I didn't say anything, so he went on. "We used to go out last year, but it didn't work out."

"Why not?"

"After a while there wasn't anything to talk about. I mean, she's pretty and all. A lot of guys would like to go out with her because she's kind of mysterious and exotic. At first. I guess that's kind of the problem with Mariah."

"Too many guys like her?"

"Not that. It's just, well, she's not that special once you get to know her." He took my hand. "She's not like you, Lucy."

163

Wasn't I supposed to be over Aspen? Wasn't I supposed to be able to control how I felt about him? The one thing I wanted in the world right then was to kiss him.

"It's okay if you want to just be friends," he said, letting go of my hand. "I can do that."

"I don't know, Aspen. It's like when I'm with you other things don't matter. I have to focus on my grades and go to work and keep Mom on track and help Jimmy." Suddenly I felt overwhelmed, and my eyes flooded with tears. "When I'm with you, I forget my responsibilities. I mean, just look at me now. All of a sudden I'm a mess."

"I don't mean to make you a mess," Aspen said. He had such a disturbed look on his face that I had to smile.

"No, it's not your fault. It's me. I just let you become too important."

"And that's a bad thing?"

"I don't know." I wiped my eyes. "Everything is so uncertain. And now we don't even have St. Agatha's. It's like I can't count on anything anymore."

"I don't want to make demands on you, I just want to be with you." He pulled a purple leaf off a branch and tucked it behind my ear. "I really miss you, Lucy."

"I miss you too," I said, and he put his arms around me. "I have missed you so much."

With Aspen's arms around me, his chin resting gently on the top of my head, I felt nested in the tree house, like everything would be fine. And that's what scared me.

20

Most of the damage to St. Agatha's had been caused by smoke and water. Only Tina's room had any structural problems—the window and part of the roof would have to be repaired.

"It still smells pretty nasty," Rachel said as we walked upstairs. "The carpet will have to be replaced, and some of your things are ruined, but on the whole we were pretty lucky."

The floor squished soggily under our feet, and the walls were dingy with smoke. A work crew had already started pulling up the carpet in some of the rooms, and volunteers had signed up to repaint the walls. Rachel handed me a black plastic trash bag.

"In a few days it should be pretty much back to normal," she said as Mom opened the drawers and closet. "Except for the smell. That might take a while."

I pulled my portfolio out from under the bed and found my ring. I put it on my left hand and flashed it at Mom.

"It's safe?" she asked, and I nodded. "But look at your artwork. Oh, Lucy, I'm so sorry." Most of the work in my portfolio was wet and smeared. The sketch of the tower and someone drowning in a river of hair was a complete blur. I balled it up and stuffed it in the black trash bag.

"I can always draw more pictures," I said, but seeing my work ruined gave me a weird lost feeling.

Jan stuck her head in the door. "How's it look in there?"

"Some of it's worth saving," Mom said, pulling soggy clothes out of the closet. "How's Tina?"

"She'll have to wear bandages for a while," Jan said.

"But she'll be okay?"

"Physically, yeah. Mentally? They're going to keep her for a couple of weeks for observation," Jan said. "Of course, charges will probably be filed."

"You mean she might go to jail?" I asked.

"Unless she gets a good lawyer," Jan said.

"She needs help, not prison," Mom said. "What about Alonzo?"

"He's with me for the time being," Jan said. "CPS wanted to put him in foster care, but Tina signed a voluntary placement form a while back. It designates me custodian."

"For how long?"

"Couple of weeks. If I had my own place, it might be longer. I'm on three waiting lists, but nothing's moving very fast."

"At least he'll have some stability for a while," Mom said.

"We'll just take it a day at a time" Jan said.

"That's about all anybody can do."

Later that day Elton dropped Crystal and Chelsea Rose off. They'd stayed with his parents, and I couldn't wait to find out how it had gone.

"His mom wasn't exactly Miss Hospitality, but it was okay," she said. "They put me and Chelsea Rose on the foldout sofa in the living room. Elton snuck down in the middle of the night for a little while." She grinned. "So you spent the night with Aspen?"

"Not *with* Aspen," I said. "At his house."

"So are you guys going out again or what?"

"Technically?"

"Come on, Lucy."

"Honestly, I don't know," I said. "But it was good to be with him again. I kind of missed him."

"No shit!" Crystal said. "About time you figured that one out."

"It's just that I don't know what I can trust."

"You can trust Aspen," Crystal said.

"But what if it doesn't work out?"

"Jeez! Why look for trouble? Don't worry so much about later that you forget about now."

Easier said than done, I thought. But she had a point.

By late afternoon most of the residents had moved back into St. Agatha's. Although it was against regulations, Paula said we could sleep with the windows open because of the dampness and the lingering smell.

I fell into bed at eight exhausted, and went straight to

sleep. By five I was wide awake. The open windows let in the faintest gray light, the sound of birds and the cool morning air. I slipped a sweatshirt over my nightgown and pulled the comforter off my bed. Taking my sketchbook, I went out into the courtyard. Wrapped in the comforter, I sat on top of a table and sketched a house built among the branches of a gigantic tree. Birds of all sizes and colors sat among the leaves. When I finished, I lay down and fell asleep and dreamed about being a bird.

By the end of the week everything was pretty much back to normal. Even the smell was gone, or maybe we were just getting used to it. The upstairs had been recarpeted and painted, the blinds had been replaced. The biggest loss was the furniture in the living room, which all had to be thrown out. Although the furniture had been ugly as a baboon's ass, as Crystal put it, it had served a purpose. Now all we had were a couple of donated couches that were even worse.

When I got home from work Friday afternoon, the kitchen was buzzing.

"What's all the excitement?" I asked, afraid of another disaster. But everyone was smiling, almost giddy with whatever was going on.

"Your mom is planning a fund-raiser," Crystal said. Mom pulled a pan of brownies out of the oven and smiled.

"She's what?"

"She's got Rachel and Paula almost convinced. They're even talking about dates. It's an assignment she has to do for school."

"Your assignment is to hold a fund-raiser?" I asked Mom.

"No, no, it's to *plan* a banquet," Crystal explained. "She doesn't have to really pull it off for the assignment. All she has to do is the paperwork for that, but she's decided we should go for it. You know, raise money for St. Agatha's."

"Because of the fire," Tatyana explained. She was crocheting an olive green receiving blanket. "To place refurnishings."

"Replace the furniture," Mom corrected. She turned to me, and I could see the same glimmer in her eyes that she used to get when she planned one of her big parties.

"It's going to be quite posh," Crystal said, adopting a snooty accent. "All the hoity-toity society people will be on hand."

Mom ignored her. "If Rachel and Paula okay it, we'll shoot for late June. I'll be out of school by then, and the weather should be nice enough to use the courtyard."

"You're going to have it here?"

"Where else? It's free. Plus it will be good PR."

"The place may be free, but how will you pay for everything else?" Since the fire St. Agatha's had no money for extras.

"Donations." She pulled several pieces of paper out of her apron pocket. "These are the businesses I'll contact. And here's the major-donors list. And here's a tentative menu."

Jimmy raced into the kitchen, followed by Alonzo and Carlos. In a minute Jan came in after them, out of breath.

"They're a handful," she said. "And they got spring fever bad! Those brownies ready?"

Mom cut the brownies and handed them around. Not that the boys needed any sugar; they were already bouncing off the walls. But Mom was in a great mood. Totally permissive.

"I'll take them down to the park," I said.

"I'm going with you." Crystal took a brownie in each hand. "I've got spring fever too, and I've been stuck here all day."

The late afternoon air was cool and the park was full of lilac and bleeding heart, leopard's bane and iris. The same kind of plants that I'd watched bloom in Andover Hills only a year ago. As the boys ran ahead with a plastic baseball and bat, Crystal and I sat down on the grass. Chelsea Rose pulled up on Crystal's shoulder and stood on plump, shaky legs. She wore a pair of pink sandals that Crystal had absolutely gone crazy over when she found them in the clothing room.

"She'll be walking before you know it," Crystal said. "But not before I get my GED."

"When are you going to take the test?" I asked.

"Tuesday. You know, two years ago I wouldn't have believed I'd care about this so much."

"You'll do great."

"Yeah, I'll pass. I've studied enough, that's for sure. It's just that sometimes I wish I could have done all this in a different order."

"How do you mean?"

"The normal way. You know, get high school out of the

way, maybe go to college. *Then* get married. *Then* have a baby. I'll only be thirty-four when Chelsea Rose graduates from high school."

"Thirty-four seems plenty old to me," I said. "And you and Elton will have half a dozen other kids by then."

"Ha!" Crystal rolled her eyes. "No more than we can send to college someday. It's just that once you make one choice, it closes off so many others."

"Don't tell me you'd give up Chelsea Rose."

"God, no. But still. You can't help but wonder. Like me and Elton might have started a band. We might have gone off to college together."

"You can still do that! You've gotten some of the hardest stuff behind you. You're totally committed to making it work," I said. "A lot of people would be jealous of that."

"Like you?" She looked at me slyly.

"Maybe," I said. "Just a little."

21

saw the envelope before Mom did. It lay in our cubby-hole in the office, with a note from Rachel about the fund-raiser. We never got mail, so any letter caught my attention. Especially a personal letter like this one. The small envelope was gray, the paper thin and expensive-looking. The address was written in blue ink.

"Looks important," Crystal said. She had come up behind me without my hearing her. Quickly I turned the envelope facedown and slipped it back into the cubbyhole.

"Who's it from?" she asked.

"How should I know?" I said. But I did. Though there was no name included, I had recognized the return address immediately.

"You liar! If you didn't know who it was from, you

wouldn't be hiding it." She pulled the envelope out of the cubbyhole again.

"That, I believe, is a federal offense," I said.

"What? Tampering with other people's mail? I've done worse." She looked at the return address, then looked at me, her mouth open in disbelief.

"Oh my God! It's from her, isn't it?" she asked.

"Yeah."

"We could take it down to the kitchen and steam it open," Crystal suggested.

"Or we could leave it here where it belongs." I took the gray envelope out of her hand and slid it back into the cubbyhole.

"Don't you want to know what it says?" she asked.

"Of course I do. But I'm not going to screw things up again because of Kathy Halperin," I said. "Besides, Mom will tell me anything I need to know."

"Or not," Crystal said. "Maybe it's a big fat check."

"Or not," I said, rolling my eyes. "Isn't it time you started minding your own business?"

Crystal grinned. "Why start now?"

Mom didn't mention the letter that night, though she'd had plenty of time to read it. After she left to drive Tatyana to her Lamaze class, I looked through her desk drawer; I didn't find it. Nor was it hidden in her purse or under her clothes in the chest of drawers. I snooped through her things pretty thoroughly, feeling both guilty and somehow justified. Then I waited two days. And then I said something.

"There was a letter in our box the other day. Did you open it?"

"I did," Mom said. She dumped a basket of clean laundry on the bed, and we started folding clothes.

"And?"

Mom looked at me steadily. "It was addressed to me, I believe."

"I know it was from Kathy," I said.

"Did you open my mail?" she asked.

"No. I recognized the address." I took one end of a bedsheet and helped Mom fold it. "So what did it say?"

Mom sighed. "Not that it's any of your business, but she wrote a condolence note."

"About Dad? Ten months after the funeral she says she's sorry?" I asked. "How did she get this address?"

"Her husband is a lawyer, Lucy. I imagine some intern in his office managed to find me."

"Did she say anything else?"

"Can't we talk about this later?" Mom asked. "I need to get these clothes put away and finish my homework and see Rachel about table linens for the banquet and get Jimmy ready for bed. All in the next two hours."

"Okay, okay." I was quiet for a couple of minutes, but the whole thing bugged me. "Why shouldn't I know what she said?"

"There's nothing to know. Kathy wrote to express her sympathy and suggested we might try to see each other."

"You're kidding! Are you going to?" Maybe Kathy had changed her mind since March. Maybe she was reaching out.

"Why should I?" Mom asked.

"Mom! She might be able to help us out of here."

"We'll be out of here soon without her help. And then we can start over without being indebted to her."

"But don't you think you should write her back? Don't you owe it to her?"

Mom threw down the shirt she was folding and put her hands on her hips. "I owe Kathy absolutely nothing. And don't you forget that, ever."

"You need to read that letter," Crystal said when I had described my conversation with Mom.

"It's not going to do any good," I said, though I was almost obsessed with knowing what it said. Crystal and I were in room 12 by ourselves, a rare event. We were listening to some CDs on Crystal's ancient boom box while Chelsea Rose napped on the double bed. She lay flat on her stomach, arms and legs thrown out. In her yellow sleeper she looked like a gold star.

"But don't you think you have a right to know? I mean, you're the one who got in touch with her in the first place."

"Yeah, and a lot of good it did," I said.

"You don't know if it did any good or not until you see the letter," Crystal said.

I hadn't thought of it quite like that. If I hadn't gone to Seattle, Kathy probably never would have written to Mom. It was obvious that the letter wasn't just a sympathy note. It was really about something else. Maybe Crystal was right. Maybe I should know what the letter said.

"Where would somebody hide a letter . . . ?" Crystal wondered aloud, and gazed around the room.

"Don't even start," I warned. But she already had.

"Did you check her underwear drawer?"

I nodded, reluctant to admit I'd been snooping.

"Did you check under the mattress?"

"That only happens in old movies," I said. "But yes."

Crystal carefully opened the desk drawer.

"I already looked there too," I said.

She opened the closet and stood in front of it with her arms crossed, thrumming her fingers against her elbow. "Where would nobody ever look . . . ?" she murmured. She pulled a Tampax box off the top shelf and examined it. She stuck her hand in Mom's boots. Then she snapped her fingers and pulled Mom's business math book off the shelf. It hadn't been opened since Mom had flunked the course. Crystal flipped through the pages. There, stuck in the section on taxes, were thin gray sheets of notepaper.

"Your mom's pretty slick." Crystal handed the book to me. "That's one long letter," she said as I slid the notepaper from between the pages.

"It's more than one." I looked at each of the thin gray sheets. There were three letters in all, the first dated only a week or so after the trip to Seattle. Kathy had been in touch with Mom for a couple of months.

"You want me to leave?" Crystal asked with a sudden, uncharacteristic sense of my need for privacy.

"No, it's okay." Just as suddenly, I wanted her to be there.

The first letter was short. *Dear Cindy,* it began, *I was terribly sorry to hear about Jim's death. My thoughts and prayers* are with you and your children. Please let me know if I can help in any way. Sincerely, your sister, Kathy.* She had added her phone number in a PS.

The second letter was dated three weeks later.

"*Dear Cindy,*" I read aloud. "*I had hoped to hear from you, but I guess that was expecting too much after so many years. I'll get straight to the point. I was first made aware of your current situation through a source I'd rather not name.*"

"That would be you," Crystal said.

"I guess so." I went on, "*In light of the circumstances I would like to offer my assistance.*"

" 'In light of the circumstances,' 'offer my assistance'— Jeez, you think she always talks like that?" Crystal asked.

"Would you let me finish?" I continued reading, "*I hope we can put our differences behind us for the sake of your children. Please let me know if I can be of assistance.*"

"You think your mom wrote her back?" Crystal asked.

I skimmed over the third letter. "Sounds like it. Listen to this: *Dear Cindy, I was pleased to receive your letter. However, you can imagine my disappointment at your re-fusal. Wilson and I are more than able to help. In fact, Wilson insists upon it.*"

"Oh, *Wilson* insists. I'm sure that went over real well with your mom," Crystal said sarcastically.

"*Please consider your children. Even temporary disadvan-tage can have long-lasting effects on the lives of young people.*" At the end of the letter she gave her phone number and asked Mom to call her.

"Do you think they talked?"

"I don't know." I flipped through the pages again,

looking for an answer. Was this the last letter? Had they talked on the phone?

"We better put these back," Crystal said, pulling me out of my thoughts. "Your mom will be home any minute."

Mom never mentioned Kathy's offer. Instead, she threw herself into planning the banquet. She was out of school until July, and with all As on her report card she was feeling like she could conquer the world. Tatyana had finished Lamaze and her first session of ESL classes, so Mom didn't have to drive her around anymore. Tatyana was huge and spent most of her time sitting around knitting and waiting for the baby to come. She had made a dozen little blankets and sweaters and a bunch of caps and booties. When I asked her how she managed to get so many made, she smiled and said. "I sleep. I eat. I make small clothing. That is all."

Mom picked Jimmy up from day care early each day, and he spent most afternoons at the park with Carlos and Alonzo, who was still living with Jan. Maybe CPS had decided it was okay. Maybe they had just forgotten about him.

With school out I was working full-time. It wasn't the most exciting way to spend summer vacation—last June we were on Maui—but money was money, and I had lots of time to draw. I had started a series of winged people. Not fairies and not angels. I didn't know where they were coming from, but they kept showing up in my sketchbook.

I had also started portraits of Carlos and Alonzo, sketching them while they watched movies on Friday nights. I hoped to be finished by the time Jan left St. Agatha's. She had applied for a job at the Feather Stone School for Native American kids north of town, and she was next on the waiting list at Brookridge Apartments, a subsidized complex that a lot of St. Agatha's residents moved into. Things were looking good for Jan. And that gave me hope.

22

One day around lunchtime Aspen showed up at the store with a chai tea and a bagel.

"Thought you might be hungry," he said, and put the bagel on the counter.

"Thanks, but I'm okay," I said. As far as I knew, Mariah's college boyfriend was back in town and she wasn't hanging with Aspen anymore. Not even as friends. Still, it bothered me the way he'd been so quick to hook up with her in the first place.

"Oh, come on," he said. "I bought blueberry just for you."

"I guess I could eat half of it," I said, falling for his smile like I always did and trying not to let it show. "You can have the other half."

Aspen pulled the bagel apart and took a sip of tea. "Can we split this too?" he asked.

"You bought it." I fidgeted with the gel pen display beside the cash register. "So how's work?"

"Hard, but the pay's good. Plus, I'm getting muscles." He pulled up his shirtsleeve and flexed. I poked his arm with my finger.

"Oooh, I'm so impressed," I teased. But I was. Since school had let out, he'd been mowing lawns and cleaning pools. His skin was golden tan and his arms were hard and lean. I wanted to touch him again. Instead I took a bite of bagel and picked up the cup of tea.

"You and your mom need any help with the party?" he asked.

"The banquet? How'd you hear about that?"

"Ann read about it in some newsletter she gets. She said your mom's in charge."

"Yeah. And life's been totally insane for the past few weeks."

"I'd be glad to give you a hand."

"I'll check. I'm sure we could find some use for your muscles."

Aspen struck a bodybuilder pose, and I laughed. The counter stayed between us the whole time he was there, and neither of us even looked in the direction of the stockroom. When he left, I didn't know whether to feel pleased at the way things had gone or disappointed.

"Jan got the job!" Crystal said when I got home.

"At Feather Stone? That's wonderful." I gave Jan a hug.

"And more," Tatyana said. "She has room."

"She got the apartment at Brookridge," Mom explained.

"Whoa, when did all this happen?"

"A unit opened up day before yesterday," Jan said. "I'll be leaving tomorrow."

I looked at Mom. She was happy for Jan, but I knew she was a little envious too. So was I. If only she would let Kathy help out. We could be in an apartment too. We could have our own bathroom and our own kitchen. I could have my own bedroom—then I stopped myself. I felt like a traitor. Mom was doing okay now, wasn't she? And I was making money and Jimmy was doing well. It would just take a little more time.

"That's fabulous," I said, trying to stay happy for Jan.

"And best of all, she can take Alonzo with her," Crystal said. "CPS granted her temporary custody."

"Well, this certainly calls for a celebration." Mom pulled a bottle of sparkling cider out of the refrigerator. "I always keep some on hand." I remembered how she kept bottles of cold champagne at our house in Andover Hills because, as she said, you never knew when you might need it. She poured the sparkling cider into mismatched glasses, and we toasted Jan's good luck.

Early the next morning we loaded Jan's things into a truck Elton had borrowed from the auto parts store where he worked.

"We'll be sleeping on the floor for a while," Jan said as she tossed sleeping bags into the back. "But at least we have a roof over our heads."

"Your very own roof," Mom said, smiling bravely. "You sure you don't need some help moving in?"

"There's not much to move," Jan said. "The boys'll help out."

"Here's a little housewarming gift." Mom held out a pound cake she'd baked the night before. "We sure will miss having you around."

"I'm only a few blocks away," Jan said, taking the cake from her. "And I'll be back on Saturdays." Once a resident left, she was expected to put in some time volunteering. Jan would help out in the office on weekends.

We waved as Jan, Carlos and Alonzo squeezed into the truck cab with Elton. It was a tight fit, but with Alonzo on Jan's lap they managed to get the door closed and drive away. It was hard to be left behind.

"Next time you see him hauling a load of stuff out of that driveway, it'll be ours," Crystal said, and quickly wiped her cheek.

Rachel met us at the door as we headed back inside. "You two want to do me a favor?" she asked.

"Sure," I said. I wasn't in the mood for chores, but I couldn't really say no.

"What's the favor?" Crystal asked, and narrowed her eyes.

"Always the cautious one, aren't you, Crystal?" Rachel said. "Come on and I'll show you." We followed her to the basement. "It's just sorting through some new donations."

"Whoa, did somebody die or something?" Crystal asked when Rachel pointed to eight large moving boxes shoved into a corner of the clothing room.

"As a matter of fact, yes. Mrs. Alma Watson, one of our biggest donors. She was eighty-seven. Her daughter delivered these yesterday. I'm afraid she didn't bother to go through any of them herself. From what I can tell some of the stuff's pretty old."

Crystal held up a beaded cashmere sweater. "Looks ancient."

"Very fifties." I ran my finger across the beadwork. "But it's beautiful, isn't it?"

"I prefer my clothes new," Crystal said. "Vintage sucks."

"Just toss anything that's not usable. And take what you want. If you get through all these boxes, you deserve whatever you like," Rachel said as she left the room.

I put the beaded sweater aside and rummaged through a box. "Is this too old-fashioned for you?" I asked Crystal, and held up a sheer blue nightgown with wide lace trim. It looked like something from 1930s Hollywood.

"Wouldn't Elton love me in this?" She held the nightgown up to her chest. "This one I'll take. You see any more?"

"About two dozen, it looks like," I said, sinking my hands into the silky material. "Mrs. Alma Watson must have had a thing for lingerie."

"Or Mr. Watson," Crystal said.

By the time we were finished, Crystal had filled a large bag with silk and satin nightgowns and slips. I'd snagged a couple of sweaters and a pink velvet dress. It was princess cut with a full skirt, midfifties, I'd guess.

"We made a pretty good haul," Crystal said as we lugged the bags upstairs. "That Alma Watson sure knew how to shop. I think she'll be my new role model."

"Role model?"

"Yeah, get rich, buy clothes, die old," Crystal said. "I could do a lot worse."

Without Jan, Carlos and Alonzo, St. Agatha's seemed a lot less noisy. It also seemed a lot more dull. So I was glad

184

when Carlos and Alonzo showed up at the door of room 12 early one morning.

"Can J-man come over?" they asked Mom as soon as she opened the door.

"How did you two get here?" she demanded. She was still in her bathrobe. "Where's your mother?"

"We walked," the boys said at the same time.

"All the way from Brookridge? By yourselves?"

Carlos and Alonzo looked at each other and shrugged. "Mama said be careful, and we were," Carlos said.

"Can I go?" Jimmy asked timidly.

"I'll walk him over there," I said, before she could say no. "I want to see Jan anyway."

"Well, I guess it's okay this time, if Lucy goes with you," Mom told Jimmy.

I pulled the portraits of Alonzo and Carlos out from under my bed. Linda had helped me mat and frame them in a nice sage green. They were wrapped in brown paper and masking tape.

"Who's that for?" Alonzo asked.

"It's a housewarming gift for Jan."

"Like a heater?"

"Not exactly," I said, and rubbed his curly head. "But it will make the apartment seem warmer, you'll see."

As we made our way down the wide shaded sidewalks toward Brookridge Apartments, I could see why Jan wasn't worried about the boys walking by themselves. The two intersections we crossed were controlled by stoplights, and the traffic was slow.

When we got to Jan's apartment, she was painting the living room walls a light cinnamon brown. A small couch draped with a green and brown striped blanket stood in the middle of the floor. Otherwise the room was empty.

"Might as well make the walls look good, since there's not much to go inside them yet." She rested the paint roller in its pan. "I'm hitting the yard sales this weekend. You want to come?"

"Maybe," I said. "Here's something for you to hang on the walls once they dry." I handed her the pictures. She tore the brown paper off Carlos's portrait and held it at arm's length.

"Lord, would you look at that! It's Carlos up and down!" she said, and unwrapped the picture of Alonzo. "These pictures look just like the boys. Look here, Carlos, Alonzo."

"It's us!" Carlos said. "Look, J-Man, it's me and Lonzo."

As the boys admired their portraits, Jan poured me a Coke and opened a bag of Cheetos. "Tell me the news," she said as we settled down on the couch.

"You just left last week." I laughed. "Nothing's changed, except it's a lot quieter."

"Yeah. I sure miss everybody. Used to be I could have a good conversation anytime I wanted to. Carlos and Alonzo, they talk all the time, but it's not the same."

"Well, they are only seven," I said.

"Tatyana had that baby yet?" Jan asked.

I shook my head. "We'll let you know when she does."

"How's Cindy's party going?"

"Right on schedule. She's getting some of the food prepared."

"Already?"

"It's only five days away," I said. "She made some rolls and other stuff that will keep in the freezer until then."

"You tell Cindy I'll be there Saturday morning to help her out."

"She's planning on it. You and Tatyana and Yolanda will be in the kitchen. I'll be serving with Ruthanne and Marie. Rachel and Paula will take care of the guests."

"And that boyfriend of yours, the one whose house you stayed at. He'll be around to set up?"

"He's not my boyfriend," I said, blushing. "But yeah, Aspen will be there."

"Are Elton and Crystal still planning on singing?"

"They've been practicing over at Elton's every night for a week."

"His parents don't mind?"

"I think since the fire they've decided to give Crystal a chance," I said. "Plus they adore Chelsea Rose."

"I guess Crystal's decided to give them a chance too," Jan said. "It works both ways."

"Yeah, it does. So how's Feather Stone?" I asked.

"The kids are great. The staff is great. I'm thinking about enrolling Carlos next year, but we'll see. It kind of depends on where Lonzo ends up. They won't take kids without Indian heritage, which is a shame. But that's how they get their federal grants."

I hung around helping Jan paint until we had finished the living room and the small kitchen. Then I pulled Jimmy away from some complicated game involving action figures and we walked home.

• • •

When we got back to St. Agatha's, Mom was in the kitchen showing Ruthanne and Marie how to wait tables.

"Come here, Lucy," she said. "Sit at the table and let them practice."

I sat down to a full place setting and let Ruthanne pretend to pour water into my glass while Marie lifted empty dishes over and over again until she had done it gracefully enough to suit my mother. Then Ruthanne sat down and let me practice.

"Serve from the left, remove from the right, pour water from the right," Mom repeated.

"Can I do it?" Jimmy asked.

"Not this time. But in a few years I'm sure I'll be able to use you," Mom said, and winked at me, as though we shared some kind of secret.

"You think Aspen would be our maitre d'?" she asked.

"Aspen will probably do whatever you want," I said.

"He'll have to dress up," she said.

I had a sudden image of Aspen in a tux, with his dreadlocks and eyebrow ring. It wasn't pretty, but whatever Mom wanted, we'd have to give it to her. It was her night.

23

The day of the banquet was beautiful. Jan and Aspen showed up around ten to help us start transforming St. Agatha's living room and courtyard. We moved the couches down to the basement and set up a dozen round tables. We put three more tables in the courtyard and took the doors off their hinges so people could move in and out easily. The tables were covered with white tablecloths, and in the center of each stood an arrangement of deep red and yellow roses. At about noon a van drove up and a man with gray hair and glasses got out and rang the call box.

"There's Roger," Mom said, and smoothed her apron as Rachel buzzed him in.

I don't know what I had expected, but Roger looked incredibly average. He was older, smaller, grayer than my father had been. He didn't seem like Mom's type at all.

After she introduced him to everyone, we helped him unload boxes of dishes, glasses and flatware from the van. A caterer Roger knew had loaned them for the weekend. Jan began folding cloth napkins that were the same burgundy red as the roses.

"Your mother sure pays attention to details," she said. "This place is going to look great."

By five o'clock everything was ready. Elton and Crystal had set up their mikes in a corner near the courtyard door so that they could be heard inside and outside. Aspen changed into a white dinner jacket and slacks donated for the occasion by Mr. Tux. He looked very nice, his golden skin set off by the crisp white jacket, and I told him so. So did Ruthanne and Marie, who raised their eyebrows at me in approval. We wore black pants and white shirts. Crystal had gone upstairs to change a while ago, and I went to find her.

"I'm almost ready," she called when I knocked on her door.

"Can't I come in?" I asked, jiggling the doorknob. Crystal flung the door open and struck a pose right out of a thirties Hollywood musical.

"Whoa, you look great!" I said. She had on one of the nightgowns we'd found in Mrs. Alma Watson's donations. It was pale gold satin, and it fit her perfectly.

"You don't think it's too revealing?" she asked. "I mean it *is* lingerie."

"Not at all. It looks like an evening dress." The gown fit tight to the waist, then began to flare to the floor. It looked more like something Ginger Rogers would have danced in than something Alma Watson slept in.

"You wearing your tiara?" I asked.

She shook her head. "Tonight I'm not a rock queen, I'm serenading the rich donors with jazz and lite rock, that's L-I-T-E. I don't think they'd get the tiara."

When we came back downstairs, Aspen was greeting guests and directing them to the courtyard for hors d'oeuvres and mocktails. Mom had wanted to serve real wine, but Rachel wouldn't budge from the no-alcohol policy. If St. Agatha's residents were expected to stay clean and sober, the donors could certainly give up wine for one evening. So Mom had gotten a grocery store to donate several cases of nonalcoholic wine. She wasn't going to sacrifice presentation and atmosphere, even if the wine was just fancy grape juice. I picked up a platter of stuffed mushrooms and walked out into the courtyard. The crowd, mostly women with a sprinkling of older men, was dressed in everything from party clothes to churchy-looking suits. I recognized a couple of faces, but no one I had actually known in my former life, which was a relief. As I passed around the mushrooms, I kept my eyes down and fixed my face like the faces of waiters in nice restaurants, completely expressionless. "You are only a moving hors d'oeuvre tray," Mom had instructed us.

It wasn't until I held the platter out to a slim woman in a blue dress and she spoke to me that I realized who she was.

"Lucy?" Kathy Halperin took a mushroom and sipped

from her wineglass. "It's nice to see you." She was perfectly composed, but I nearly dropped the platter.

"Y-You too," I stammered, my face burning. The cold afternoon in Seattle came back to me. The way she had pushed me out of her house. The shock and disappointment. My first impulse was to dump the tray on her pointy black shoes. Instead I just stood there while she carefully chose another mushroom.

All of a sudden I understood why Mom didn't want her help. For months I'd been hoping that Mom would swallow her pride and let Kathy take control of our situation. I hadn't realized that pride was the only thing Mom had left. If Kathy made things right, what would that leave Mom with?

"Your mother has done a wonderful job," Kathy said, nodding at the beautifully set tables.

"Thanks," I said. What was she doing here? Mom had told her no!

"Does she know you're here?" I asked.

"I think I'll wait and surprise her later," she said. "You won't spoil it, will you?"

Before I could answer, Crystal appeared and told me to report to the kitchen. I excused myself, then followed Crystal back through the courtyard. Once inside, I grabbed her and pulled her into the stairwell.

"Do you know who that was?" I hissed.

"Of course. Why do you think I rescued you? She looks just like her pictures." Crystal took the tray of mushrooms from my unsteady hands. "So what'd she say?"

"She's planning to surprise Mom!"

"Cindy doesn't need any surprises. You should tell her."

"I was planning to. But what if it throws her into a panic?"

"What if she steps out of the kitchen and runs into her? Which would be worse? Private meltdown or public cardiac arrest?"

"You're right." I took the tray of mushrooms and headed toward the kitchen.

"Where have you been?" Mom snapped as soon as I came through the door. "Ruthanne and Marie have already started serving salads." She jerked a pan of rolls out of the oven and handed them to Tatyana, who put them in bread baskets. She was a lot more keyed up than I'd expected, and for a moment I was afraid she wouldn't be able to pull it off. Now was definitely not the time to introduce Kathy into the mix.

"Take this tray. And tell Marie to serve from the left, the left."

I served the salads to a table full of well-tanned fifty-year-olds laughing and whispering like middle-school girls. Crystal and Elton were performing some jazz standards and the crowd was loving it. Someone had put out a wineglass for tips, and it was already full. Kathy was sitting at the farthest table with her back toward the door, apparently trying to stay inconspicuous. Just don't move, I silently pleaded.

Back in the kitchen Mom was in high gear. Her hair was stuck to her forehead, and she was barking orders to Jan and Tatyana. Roger was washing dishes. I'd just have to hope Kathy stayed put until after dessert and coffee were served.

For the next hour we were incredibly busy serving up

chicken cordon bleu with wild rice and asparagus, brewing coffee, filling wineglasses and water glasses. Once he had seated everyone, Aspen picked up the slack wherever he could. I felt him watching me and I caught his eye. He winked. Mom never left the kitchen. She was just torching the tops of the crème brûlée when Marie came in and told her Rachel wanted her to come out and say something.

"I look like a dishrag," Mom said, looking at her reflection in a pot top. She fluffed up her hair and took off her apron. "But I'm not here to impress people with my looks. Tell Rachel I'll be out in a second."

I poured her a glass of cold water and she drank it in one gulp.

"You look fine," Roger said, and gave her shoulder a little squeeze. Mom took a deep breath and went through the door. After Elton played a short fanfare on the guitar, Rachel introduced Mom as the mastermind behind the banquet and gave a little speech about how wonderful she had been. Mom ducked her head and smiled as the room broke into applause.

"She's a natural," Roger said as he clapped enthusiastically. "I don't know when I've had a student as good at kitchen management and as artistically talented as your mother. She's a rare bird."

"I'm glad you think so," I said absently. I wasn't really interested in what he thought of Mom. I was too busy looking for Kathy, who had left her table. Where was she? Was she going to ambush Mom as soon as she finished her little speech? I waited, hardly breathing, until Mom came back into the kitchen. Marie and Ruthanne were circulating around the tables with coffeepots. Without a word Aspen took the tray of crème brûlée I was supposed to be serving and walked out into the dining area.

"Mom, we need to talk," I said. She had finally sat down and was devouring a salad like she hadn't eaten in days.

"If it's about Kathy, I spotted her as soon as she got here," she said with her mouth full of baby greens.

"You did?"

"After the letters I thought she might show up. It's the sort of thing she'd do."

"Letters?" I asked innocently.

"She wrote me three times. Called twice. Actually, it's been good. We needed to talk, but I'm still not taking her money. I know you don't understand, Lucy."

"I think I do," I said.

"Do you?" Mom looked at me intently, and I nodded. Mom buttered a roll. "I expect she'll make a scene of some sort before she leaves."

"What do you mean, a scene?"

"Offer me money in front of people, something like that. She thinks I won't be able to say no then. It wouldn't look right, and Kathy always did put a lot of emphasis on looks." Mom quickly wiped her mouth and smoothed her hair. "What did I tell you? Here she comes now."

Kathy hurried toward Mom with her hands outstretched. She took Mom gingerly by the shoulders, as if she were afraid she'd get crème brûlée on her blue dress.

"Cindy, the banquet was just lovely."

Mom thanked her as I started carrying dirty plates to the sink.

"What a wonderful event," Kathy said. "Now that it's over, it's time to start thinking about the future."

"Thanks again, Kathy," Mom said. "But I'm staying here."

"Can't we at least discuss it?"

"We have discussed it," Mom said.

Kathy nodded, but she wasn't giving up. "This really isn't a good time, is it? I'm staying at the Davenport. Why don't we meet for lunch there tomorrow? At noon? Bring the children."

Mom hesitated, then said we'd be there.

"Why can't she just take no for an answer?" I asked Mom as we washed dishes.

"That's Kathy. She has to have her way," Mom said, then added, "I think she really is concerned about you and Jimmy. She might be selfish and domineering, but Kathy's not all bad."

"It was a great party," Aspen said to Mom right before she went upstairs. It was after eleven, and everything was pretty much back to normal.

"I'm glad you could be part of it. You were a big help," Mom said, and I could tell she meant it.

Aspen and I walked across the street to the parking lot where he'd left his car. The air was warm and breezy and smelled like new-cut lawns. Aspen had taken off his jacket and tie. In the streetlights the white tux shirt looked lavender and his face took on deep shadows. I moved closer to him and he took my hand.

"How much did you make?" he asked, but I could tell he was thinking about something else.

"Paula said they sold every ticket. At sixty dollars a plate, I guess that's over five thousand dollars. Not bad."

"Not bad at all." Aspen smiled at me and shook his head.

"What are you thinking?" I asked.

"Nothing. No, that's not true." He looked away almost shyly. "I'm thinking I'd like to kiss you."

"Nothing ever happens by just thinking about it," I said, and leaned toward him until our lips touched.

It was happening again. I was getting wrapped up in Aspen, but it felt okay. I thought about what Crystal had said: Don't worry so much about tomorrow that you forget today. Today, now, was where I was, kissing Aspen. And it was where I wanted to be.

When I got back to our room, it was after midnight. Trying not to make any noise, I turned the doorknob carefully and let myself in. I didn't need to bother about being quiet, though. The light was on, Jimmy was sitting up in bed with a terrified look on his face and Tatyana was doubled over, her face white with pain.

"What's wrong?" I asked.

"Nothing's wrong," Mom said. "The baby's coming and I've got to get her to the hospital."

"Now?"

"These things can't wait." She slipped on some shoes and grabbed her purse. "Take Jimmy to Crystal, then wake up Paula. Tell her to call the hospital to let them know we're coming."

After Paula called, I waited by the front door with Tatyana until Mom drove up and we helped her into the car. She was doing her Lamaze breathing and sounded like a steam engine.

"Should I go too?" I asked, hoping Mom would say no. I couldn't stand being around so much pain, but I'd go if she needed me.

"You stay with Jimmy," Mom said. "Let him know everything's okay."

"What about tomorrow?" I asked, suddenly remembering our lunch date with Kathy.

"I'll call you if I can't make it," Mom said as Tatyana let out a groan. "I don't think this is going to take very long."

When I got back upstairs, I fell into bed with Jimmy and, despite all the excitement, slept like a rock until Mom came back the next morning.

"Did she have the baby?" I asked.

"A beautiful girl," Mom said. "Eight pounds, two ounces, raven black hair and blue eyes. Tatyana's doing great too."

"What's she going to name her?"

She smiled. "Cindy Luchiana."

Mom managed to get a couple hours of sleep before she had to get ready for lunch. She stood in front of the mirror and pressed the puffiness under her eyes.

"God, I *look* like I live in a shelter, don't I?" she said. "But there's nothing I can do about it now. Come on, Jimmy," she said, and smoothed down his hair. "Let's go get some lunch."

24

When we got to the restaurant, Kathy was already seated at a table beside a window. She waved and stood up to hug each of us and kiss the air next to our ears. She had on a brown linen dress and tastefully chunky jewelry. One thing about Kathy, she had style.

"Order anything you want, kids," she said as we opened the menus. Mom ordered the most inexpensive salad on the menu, and I did the same. Jimmy asked for a hamburger, no pickles, no lettuce, no tomato, no ketchup.

"And a Shirley Temple," he said, and looked at Mom to see if that was all right. She nodded.

"Bring us a bottle of the Mount Spokane Chardonnay," Kathy said, and smiled at Mom. "We should celebrate, don't you think?"

"None for me," Mom said, covering her glass with her hand.

"Oh, come on, Cindy. Relax. You're not at St. Agatha's."

When the waiter uncorked the bottle, Mom let him pour her a glass.

"To a successful banquet," Kathy said, and they clinked the rims of their glasses. Mom took a small sip and put the glass down carefully. After a few comments about last night's dinner and questions for Jimmy about what he was doing in preschool, Kathy launched into her proposal.

"I want to help you get back on your feet," she began.

"You know I won't take your money," Mom said politely. Her smile was tired but determined.

"Now, Cindy. Your children shouldn't be prevented from living a normal life just because their father didn't maintain his finances."

"Let's leave Jim out of this," Mom said firmly, and glanced at Jimmy, who was folding his napkin into a little tent for the salt and pepper shakers. "I really appreciate your offer, and I'm glad we had a chance to clear the air. But in the past week new options have opened up." I looked at Mom carefully, trying to figure out if she was making things up or if there really were options I didn't know about.

"Really?" Kathy asked, and nudged her half-eaten plate of linguini away from her. She poured herself another glass of wine. Mom's glass was still almost full.

"Starting next week I'll be managing a restaurant," Mom announced. "Renovations are finished and the owner plans to open on the twenty-fifth."

I opened my mouth, then closed it again when Mom gave me her not-one-word glance. Now wasn't the time to ask questions. Either Mom was making the whole thing up or this was what we'd been waiting for. Whichever, I was supposed to act like I knew about this already.

"Well, congratulations, Cindy. I had no idea," Kathy said. "And you'll have enough?" She raised her eyebrows.

"More than adequate," Mom said. As if Mom's salary— real or otherwise—were any of Kathy's business.

"Well. Tell me! I'm dying to hear all about it." Kathy leaned forward a little too eagerly.

"It's called Napoli and it specializes in Italian and nouvelle cuisine. It seats sixty," Mom said. "What else can I tell you?"

For a minute I almost felt sorry for Kathy. She seemed to be trying so hard.

"So, what's new with you?" I asked, feeling awkward. But it seemed to break the tension. Kathy smiled and told us all about her new springer spaniel until the waiter came with the check.

"I'll get that," Kathy said, pulling out her American Express card.

"Thanks," I said quickly. Mom didn't argue.

"Why didn't you tell me about the restaurant?" I exclaimed as we drove back to St. Agatha's.

"I wasn't sure I was ready to take such a big step," Mom said. "Not until last night went so well and I knew I could really do it."

"It's Roger's, isn't it?" I said, suddenly realizing how things had happened.

Mom nodded. "I would have told you sooner, but I

didn't want you to get your hopes up, in case things didn't work out. And there's another thing." Her tone of voice made me nervous. "We'll be leaving St. Agatha's."

"We're moving? When?" I asked, thinking of the possibilities. Our own place, our own kitchen and bathroom! Maybe my own room!

"In the next couple of weeks. As soon as we can iron out the details."

We? Did that mean Roger? My excitement melted. Were we moving in with him?

"Well, don't you want to know where we'll be living?" Mom asked when I didn't say anything.

"Sure," I said, though I was almost afraid to find out.

"I'm taking a small salary advance and putting a deposit on an apartment."

"You mean for you, me and Jimmy?"

"Who else would it be for? And it's not at Brookridge either. It's a nicer place called Riverview. I mean, Brookridge is fine, but this place will be better. At least for now." She pulled the car into St. Agatha's parking lot. "So what do you think?"

"What do you think I think!" I said. "It's absolutely wonderful!"

"Excuse me," Jimmy said from the backseat.

"What is it, Jimmy?" Mom said.

"Can I have a sleepover?"

"Of course you can," Mom said, and gave him a hug as she helped him out of the car. "As soon as we move in you can have as many sleepovers as you want."

• • •

"Why didn't you tell Kathy we'd be moving?" I asked that night before Mom turned out the light.

"I wanted to tell you and Jimmy first," she said. "I'll send her a note in a couple of days. Thank her for lunch and give her our new address."

"Do you think we'll be seeing her again?" I asked.

"Oh, I imagine we'll be on her Christmas card list, but that's probably it." Mom pressed her lips together. "I never much liked my sister. Isn't that strange?"

"Not really," I said, remembering something Jan had said once. "It's like poker. You didn't get to choose her, she's just one of the cards you were dealt. What were the chances you'd get a winning hand?"

25

The Monday before we moved I woke up to banging on the door of our room. It was only eight o'clock, but Mom had already left for work. She was spending long hours at the restaurant and loving it. Every night she brought home a Styrofoam box full of an amazing dessert or appetizer for Jimmy and me. I opened the door and found Crystal in the hallway holding up two dresses. One was yellow with lingerie straps and seed pearl beading. The other was green taffeta, strapless with a ruffled skirt.

"Which do you like better?" she asked.

"Which do I like better?" I repeated, wondering if this were a dream.

"Yeah, which." Crystal shook the dresses at me. "Are you even awake?"

"I'm not sure, but I definitely like the yellow one."

"Do you think the green one is too dark?"

"Too dark for what, Crystal? Could you maybe give me some context here?"

"For a wedding," Crystal said.

"You're going to a wedding? Whose?"

"Mine!" Crystal said. "And you're going too."

I shrieked and pulled her into our room, and we both fell over on the bed laughing. Jimmy sat up and told us to go away.

"I'm getting married, Jimbo!" Crystal said, but he just put the pillow over his head.

"When did you decide to do this?" I asked.

"About a year and a half ago."

"I know, but why today?"

"Because the timing is right. Will you go with us, Lucy? Will you be my maid of honor?"

"You know I will," I said, and hugged her.

"Okay, we need to be at the courthouse at one. It's not a big-deal church wedding, but I still want to look good."

"Go with the yellow, then. Yellow's the color of love in some cultures."

"How do you know that?" Crystal asked.

"Jan said so. It's Native American."

"Yellow it is, then," Crystal said. "Yellow for love."

The wedding was small, just Elton and Crystal, Elton's parents and me. And Chelsea Rose, of course, who stood on plump little legs holding on to Crystal's skirt. She had started walking three days before. Elton looked very handsome in a dark suit, his hair pulled back into a ponytail, his blue eyes sparkling. Crystal held a bouquet of daisies. Elton's mother couldn't stop crying, but I think it was because she was truly happy.

After the wedding we all went back to Elton's parents' house for cake and coffee. Jan and the boys joined us there. I called Mom, but she couldn't leave Napoli on such short notice. Instead she sent one of the waiters over with a giant blueberry cheesecake and a bottle of champagne. *Best Wishes from Cindy and Roger,* the card said. I guess she'd forgotten that both Elton and Crystal were underage. Or maybe she just couldn't resist the old habit of pulling a cold bottle out of the refrigerator for any celebration. Elton's parents didn't drink, not even to celebrate, so Crystal slipped the bottle into her tote bag and winked at me. "For the honeymoon," she whispered. Elton had called Aspen that morning, but he had three pools to clean and couldn't make it.

"He said if he'd known ahead of time, he'd have been here," Elton said.

"If I'd known ahead of time, I would have gotten you a wedding present," I said.

"You got six months, according to those online etiquette ladies," Crystal said. "I'll take it whenever."

"I'm sure you will," I teased her. "So will you be moving out soon?"

"Tomorrow! Elton's parents have a place on Priest Lake. It's a small place. They use it in the summer."

Everything was happening so fast. I knew moving out was what we all wanted. But I couldn't help feeling a little sad that it was time to say goodbye.

"It's a trailer," Elton said, putting his arm around Crystal. "She won't admit it, but that's what it is."

"Okay. But can we at least call it a mobile home?"

"Call it a chateau if you want," Elton said, and kissed her cheek.

"How about the Lake House? Doesn't that sound impressive?" Crystal changed into her snooty voice. "We'll be staying temporarily at the Lake House while our Realtor finds us a property."

"A property?" I laughed.

"Whatever."

"It's not forever." Elton nodded. "There's *a* property waiting out there for us somewhere."

"Nothing's forever." Crystal picked up Chelsea Rose. "Except us."

The next day I helped Crystal and Elton load up Crystal's things and the portable crib Chelsea Rose had been sleeping in. Rachel said for her to take it. She could give it back to St. Agatha's once Chelsea Rose outgrew it.

"You call me," Crystal said as she wrote her phone number on the back of my hand. "Don't wash that hand until you get it memorized."

"Okay, and I'll let you know as soon as we get a phone."

"I mean it. You better stay in touch," Crystal said.

"Crystal! Of course I will."

"I just don't want you to forget about me once your life gets all better, rich girl."

"My God, as if I *could* forget about you!"

"What's that supposed to mean?" Crystal put her hands on her hips and narrowed her eyes, and I remembered the first time I met her. "One day when I'm famous my phone number will be worth a lot."

Elton yelled at Crystal to hurry up, and she gave me a quick hug. "Call me soon," she said, and jumped into the truck next to Chelsea Rose.

It was beginning to get dark, and I wandered out to the courtyard. Ruthanne was sitting at a table smoking with Yolanda. We talked for a couple of minutes, then I went inside. The lobby looked good with its new couches and tables. Somebody had left the TV on; I turned it off and sat down. Mom was at the restaurant, Jimmy was at Jan's. Crystal was on her way to her new home. The Lake House, I thought, and smiled. I felt restless. I wandered into the kitchen and opened the refrigerator and took out a slice of cake, but that wasn't what I was looking for. What *was* I looking for?

I went into the office and dialed Aspen's phone number.

"What's up?" I said when he answered the phone.

"Lucy?"

"You want to hang out?"

"Sure!" He sounded glad I'd called.

"Can you come get me?" I asked.

"I'll be there in about half an hour. I've got to do something first. Don't go anywhere."

"Don't worry. I'll be waiting."

I went up to our room and pulled off my shirt and shorts. I took Mrs. Alma Watson's pink velvet dress out of the closet and slipped it over my head. It fit perfectly, the full skirt falling a few inches above my ankles. Then I slid my portfolio out from under my bed and found my sapphire ring. *Wear it on special occasions*, Mom had said when she gave it to me. I slipped it on my finger and watched it sparkle.

"You look great," Aspen said when he arrived. Taking my hand, he twirled me around. "What's the occasion?"

"I don't know yet," I said. "I just felt like velvet."

We drove to Aspen's house through the gathering dark. The night was warm and the stars were beginning to come out. A full moon shone yellow just above the sycamore trees.

"Wait here for a minute," Aspen said. "Better make it five, okay?"

"Okay—but why?"

"You'll see." He jumped out of the car and sprinted around the house. Inside I could see Ann reading in the lamplight. Bobby came to the open door and barked twice.

When I figured five minutes were up, I got out of the car and went in the direction Aspen had gone. A wavering line of candles lit the way across the backyard to the tree house. Although it was almost dark, I could see that the tree house was draped in thin white cloth. It glowed like a magical tent with candles lighting it up from inside. I followed the candle path, and when I got to the bottom of the ladder, Aspen stepped out of the darkness holding a single red rose.

"It's beautiful," I said. "How did you get them all lit so fast?"

"Elves," Aspen said, and handed me the rose. "After you," he added, and he followed me into the magical glowing tree house full of candles and roses. And Aspen, who smelled like cloves and leaves and summer.

So that was the beginning of it and the end. The beginning of me and Aspen and the end of St. Agatha's. Or not really the end. I still volunteer there on Sunday afternoons, taking care of kids just to give their moms a break. We've been living at Riverview for seven months and, after living in a single room for so long, a three-bedroom apartment seems like a mansion. Almost everyone we knew when we lived at St. Agatha's is gone now, except for Ruthanne and Marie.

Tatyana and her baby moved in with a Ukrainian couple she met through the Eastern Orthodox church she started attending. Mom goes to see her every now and then. Cindy Luchiana is a beautiful baby, as you might expect from such a beautiful mother. And a good mother too. Like Crystal, Mom says, Tatyana is a natural.

I see Jan pretty often, since the boys still get together and play. And I see Crystal a lot too. After spending the summer at Priest Lake, she and Elton started renting a little house not far from Riverview. Along with volunteering at St. Agatha's, Crystal's working in a music store part-time—she leaves Chelsea Rose with Elton's mom two days a week—and Elton's full-time at the auto supply store. Bogus Orange still plays on the weekends, and Crystal, the Queen of Rock, still wears her tiara and sings.

Jimmy's in kindergarten now and he's already reading. He's also the class clown, which was a surprise to Mom and me. But now that he's found his true talent, he keeps us laughing.

Napoli is one of the most popular restaurants in town, and Mom's happier than I've ever seen her. Ever. She still keeps fresh flowers on Dad's grave, but it seems like much longer than a year and a half since he died. When she talks about him now, it's kind of like she's talking about someone she knew a long time ago. She and Roger spend a lot of time together at the restaurant, and I don't know where that might lead, but wherever it goes, I'll be happy for her.

Aspen? Well, he's my best friend. I don't know what will happen when he takes off for college next fall. Whatever we've got right now probably isn't forever. We just are what we are, and it's good. As Crystal says, you can't worry so much about later that you forget about now. So we hang out in the tree house and play Frisbee with his dog and wait for the rest of our lives to happen.

BETH COOLEY is an associate professor of English at Gonzaga University in Spokane, Washington, where she lives with her husband and their two daughters. Her first novel, *Ostrich Eye*, won the Delacorte Press Prize for a First Young Adult Novel.